Santiago Toole pulled the bolt. The only reason he locked up at night was to keep drunken cowboys and opium fiends from stealing his supplies.

"Holy Mary," he muttered. That was as much an epithet as an Irish doctor banished to the New World would permit himself.

He swung the door open and lifted the lantern, intending to confront the sources of the persistent hammering and invite them in. But they didn't wait for an invitation. Three men bulled in. One wore a red bandanna over his face, its top just below his brown eyes. The other two wore Harvest Queen flour sacks over their heads, with holes gouged out for eyes, nostrils, and mouths. Water rivered off their yellow slickers.

"Holy Mary!" muttered Dr. Toole. Each of these gents had a black revolver in hand, its giant bore pointing directly at Toole's chest.

THE FATE

Richard S. Wheeler

FAWCETT GOLD MEDAL • NEW YORK

A Fawcett Gold Medal Book
Published by Ballantine Books
Copyright © 1992 by Richard S. Wheeler

Library of Congress Catalog Card Number: 91-92398

ISBN 0-449-14784-3

Manufactured in the United States of America

First Edition: June 1992

For Bruce and Sandra Prowell

Chapter 1

The persistent knocking came at the worst possible moment. Santiago Toole had just gone to bed, but he and Mimi were far from asleep. He sighed and released her. Muttering, he rolled to the edge of his bed and stabbed his feet at slippers. He missed, and the slippers skittered away like rats.

"Oh, Santo," she breathed, as disappointed and needful as he. She pulled the covers over her and giggled suddenly.

"They want a doctor," he muttered, pulling his abandoned nightshirt over him. "Whenever it rains, someone wants a doctor."

The hammering persisted, along with the clamor of male voices at the front of their calcimined cottage.

He stood in the dark, needing a little more time, clawing for his bathrobe in the inky dark. He would have to find the lantern if he wanted to get to the front door without stubbing his toes a few times.

The shouting increased. "I'm coming," Toole yelled. "Hold your bloomin' horses."

He fumbled his way from the bedroom to the parlor and from the parlor to his medical office at the front. The hammering persisted.

"Need a doc," a voice yelled.

Toole crept forward, guarding his toes against doorjambs, and found the kerosene lamp. He pulled the glass chimney off, found a lucifer, scratched it under the table. Light flared, blinding him. In a moment he had the lamp going and the chimney back on.

"Hurry up," someone yelled.

Toole muttered unhappily, not liking being torn from Mimi and her unbanked fires. Not liking a trip into a rainy night. But that was the way it went: let it rain, and someone wanted a doctor. A law of nature. The corollary was, let it rain and no one committed a crime. He'd learned that over the years. On a rainy night Sheriff Toole could go to bed early.

Doctoring in Miles City, Montana Territory, had netted him perhaps two hundred dollars a year, most of it paid in chickens, potatoes, spavined horses, and once a milch cow. So he'd become sheriff of Custer County too, eking out enough between the two jobs to survive. The town fathers had been skeptical, but found out soon enough that he could shoot lead pills from a .44 just as easily as he could set bones.

This night he'd seen the ten o'clock eastbound off, watching rain hiss from the boiler of its big four-six Baldwin. He'd watched the four-car passenger train—an express car, two coaches, and one of Pullman's hotel Palace cars—vanish in a blur of steam and wetness and buttery light. Then he'd gone home, the feel of Mimi's warm arms filling his mind.

"All right, all right!" he yelled, gliding over cold plank floors, past materia medica in green tins and paper packets and carboys.

He pulled the bolt. The only reason he locked up was to keep drunken cowboys from stealing his ardent spirits, and opium fiends from snatching his morphia and laudanum and Dover's powder.

"Holy Mary," he muttered. That was as much an epithet as an Irish doctor banished to the New World would permit himself.

He swung his door open and lifted the lantern, intending to confront the sources of the persistent hammering and invite them in. But they didn't wait for an invitation. Three men bulled in. One wore a red bandanna over his face, its top just below his brown eyes. The other two wore Harvest Queen flour sacks over their heads, with holes gouged out for eyes, nostrils, and mouths. Water rivered off their yellow slickers.

"Holy Mary!" muttered Dr. Toole. Each of these gents had a black revolver in hand, its giant bore pointing squarely at Toole's chest.

They stood there a moment, puddles collecting at their feet, eyeing Toole in his nightshirt.

"Am I being robbed?" Toole asked acidly.

"We're taking you to fix up a man," said one of the flour sacks.

"I suppose he has a migraine," Toole retorted.

He thought of dashing the lamp at their feet, starting a conflagration that would keep them hopping and permit him to escape. But that was nonsense.

"You may hand me the lantern," said the one who seemed to be the leader. "Slowly."

Something tickled Toole's mind. *You may . . .* He'd never encountered a bandit who used good grammar. He handed the lantern to the man.

"Move," the bandit said, prodding Toole toward the rear of the house.

Move toward Mimi, move toward his clothing, abandoned wherever he'd thrown it in their haste and joy. He stopped suddenly. "You realize I'm also sheriff of Custer County. And I'll chase you to the ends of the earth."

"Hurry up. Every second counts. The man's hurt."

They trotted through the parlor and down the hall while sinister shadows bobbed. They crowded into the bedroom, where the yellow light revealed Mimi sitting up in bed, her olive shoulders bare and inviting, the coverlets tucked up over her body—and a single-shot derringer in her hand.

"Put it down, madam, or your husband'll be hurt."

Santiago nodded slightly. She lowered it, fear radiating from her.

"Get dressed—and hurry."

Mortified, Toole glanced at the three armed men who'd crowded into his bedroom like an invading army. He found his britches and stepped into them, tucking his nightshirt in. He slid on his hightop boots, not bothering with stockings.

He drew a thick sweater over his nightshirt, knowing it'd be cold out there.

"I'm sorry, madam, but we'll have to embarrass you," one of the Harvest Queen flour sack said. "Roll over on your stomach. We'll have to truss you up."

Toole turned warily, hating this part of it, knowing what was coming. "I'll do it. You can spare a lady." He emphasized the last word.

"I'm sorry, Dr. Toole. And madam."

Again, the politeness. This was no ordinary bandit. Unhappily, Mimi did as she was bid, keeping the blanket over her as if it was battleship armor.

One of the flour-sack men nodded at one man. "Go." The men retreated, leaving the leader and one other. "Watch Toole; your back to Mrs. Toole," Flour Sack said.

The remaining man turned his back to Mimi but kept his revolver aimed at Toole's middle.

"My apologies, Mrs. Toole," one of the Harvest Queen men said, slowly peeling back the blanket. Mimi lay on her stomach, her slim bare back with its flawless flesh breathtaking in the yellow light. Rage boiled through Toole.

The man drew the blanket all the way off, baring all of Mimi's backside. Tears leaked from her eyes into the pillow. The utter beauty of her slender form and glowing flesh elicited a quick intake of breath in the bandit.

"I have no choice. I grieve at this insult as much as you do. Put your hands behind you."

She did. He pulled a wide thong from a pocket under his slicker and bound her wrists. Then he bound her ankles, doing a careful job of it. Mimi would never wriggle free. He pulled the blanket back over her. "Are you comfortable?" the bandit asked. "Dr. Toole will be back in a couple of hours."

She nodded in her pillow, leaking tears.

It all amazed Toole. He was oddly grateful for the man's sensitivity. "I'll be back, Mimi," he said softly.

She wept quietly from shame, immobility—and relief it hadn't been worse.

"All right," the man said, prodding Toole forward. "Get your gear. You'll be treating a serious wound in the stomach."

"A perforation made by lead no doubt," Toole snapped.

He snatched his Gladstone with its instruments and small vials of powders. He added a blue bottle of laudanum to it, and then slid into his black slicker, which hung from an antler coatrack next to his skeleton.

"I'll take your bag," Flour Sack said. "We'll blindfold you now."

The bandit slipped behind Toole. A folded bandanna suddenly blotted out his vision. He felt the man knot it tightly and then tie his hands behind him.

Toole knew it would be a hard, unbalanced ride with his hands bound behind him. They led him out. He felt the lash of cold rain, and heard it dripping and puddling. They made him stand beside a horse. He could smell the wet animal. Someone lifted one of his feet into a stirrup; others hoisted him into a dripping saddle that instantly soaked his britches and sent an icy chill into him.

He wanted some sense of where he was going, but they were ready for that. They turned his horse in a small circle several times, and when they'd finished, he hadn't the faintest idea what direction they were taking him. He knew only that four bandits, one of them unusually sensitive and well educated, were leading him through a June shower into an inky night, unseen by anyone in slumbering Miles City. And that the pattering rain would dissolve their trail through the slippery gumbo.

"Holy Mary," he muttered. This was something to awaken every instinct in a sheriff and doctor. Masked men. A robbery somewhere. A bullet wound. Which probably meant a fight—resistance during the robbery. Maybe injury and death for others. This would be only the beginning.

He had only his ears to help him, but all he heard was the splash of hooves, an occasional snort and cough of a horse, and the hawking and spitting of one of the men.

The ride seemed endless. He listened to the splashing of

hooves, waiting for something: if they crossed the military bridge over the Tongue River at the west end of town, he would hear the thump of hoofbeats on wood. But it didn't happen and he knew they were traveling south or east. The Yellowstone River, running north of Milestown, required a ferry. They didn't take the ferry, and that eliminated half the circle. Neither were they traveling west.

He felt his horse labor up steep slopes, skidding and pawing through the greasy gumbo, lurching alarmingly when it lost traction. South, then. They were climbing the southern bluffs of the Yellowstone. He'd narrowed it to less than ninety degrees. He marveled that these night riders knew the trail so well on a night so inky. They either lived in this area or had rehearsed all this.

Water trickled down his face and neck like cold iron riding his flesh. It chilled him, though the air was mild. No one spoke, and it occurred to him he might elicit some valuable information if he asked questions.

"You might tell me about the injury," he said to the men he sensed were riding beside him.

No one replied.

"I can save time—and maybe a life—if you tell me all you can about the injury in advance. I'll know better what to do," he said.

"Gunshot," someone said.

"Where exactly?"

"Lower gut."

"Which side?"

"Left, I think."

The lower left quadrant. Not much there except intestine. "How far left?"

"I don't know. We didn't look. Just tried to stop the bleeding."

"Where did it exit? Near the backbone?"

"No, it didn't hit the backbone."

"But it did exit?"

"I don't know."

"Is it bleeding?"

"Some."

There were worse places to take a shot in the abdomen. It'd probably be a slow death from peritonitis rather than a fast one from hemorrhage. All the worse for the bandit. "How long ago?"

That met with silence.

"What caliber?"

"Thirty-eight."

"Was the man conscious?"

"Rode the whole way."

"His only chance is total rest. We don't have a hospital in Miles. If you'll surrender him, I'll treat him in the jail."

Silence.

"Are others hurt?"

More silence. Toole took it for a yes. He rode through the dark, feeling rain lash his face and hands, soak his bandanna blindfold, and trickle into his boots. Shot with a .38-caliber weapon. Not a common caliber among cattlemen and range riders.

"You're aware you've abducted an officer of the law?"

"We know who you are, Sheriff Toole."

The polite one again. The one with a certain twang in his voice Toole couldn't place. He hadn't been in the United States long enough to separate the dialects. But one thing he was sure of: the polite bandit spoke with a clipped precision that spoke of education. It was no voice he'd ever heard around Milestown.

"If you want my hands to function properly when I attend your partner in crime, you'd better release them. They're numb and I can't feel a thing. Not exactly the right condition for surgery."

His horse stopped. He heard someone dismount, landing heavily in mud. He felt a knife gently sever the cords that bound his wrists behind him. He lifted his arms, trying to drive the ache from them and his shoulders. He heard the man clamber heavily into a saddle, and then his horse jerked forward again. Toole didn't possess the reins, but he didn't mind.

"If you pull off your blindfold, I'll tie them up again."

"Will you have light?"

"A coal oil lantern."

"Not enough," Toole said.

"We are visited by Fate," the man said.

They rode an endless distance through a world whipped by water. Toole judged it to be nearly two hours. Then he heard the mumble of voices. The party stopped. He was assisted off his horse and led into a building of some sort. At least through a door. Into dryness. But the temperature was no different. Someone lit a lantern. He knew that much through his blindfold. Then hands at the back of his head wrestled with the bandanna, unable to free the water-soaked knot. Someone yanked the blindfold upward, and Toole blinked in the buttery brilliance of the lantern.

"There," the polite one said, from behind his flour-sack mask.

A man curled on the floor, his head hidden in a sack, his knees drawn up and his britches soaked with brown blood. Someone handed Toole his Gladstone.

Toole knew exactly where he was. He'd been here several times. He peered at the familiar walls of the soddy and the roof of jackpine poles covered with a foot of Custer County clay. It'd been the domain of a banty Irishman named Murphy. The man had claimed a hundred sixty on a spring six miles south of Miles and raised a few sheep—until he'd vanished. He'd been harassed by cattlemen. Toole had suspected foul play and had gone over this place diligently and asked a lot of questions. But no one knew anything, and Toole had found no evidence of trouble. The soddy had been uninhabited for a year.

"You know this place," the polite one said. "That may alter our plans."

Santiago wished he'd been less obvious. He also realized this bandit chief was shrewd.

He knelt beside the wounded man. Alert eyes peered at him through the eye holes of his mask. Toole grabbed a wrist and found the pulse elevated and weak, but steady.

"Have you bled a lot?" he asked.

"A lot," the man said.

Toole doubted it. The man's color was good. "All right. I'll have a look at this," he said. He turned to the polite one. "Hold your lamp close."

The injured man's hands were soft and manicured. He had not done hard labor in his lifetime. Two high-class bandits, Toole thought as he wrestled with the man's britches.

He heard some thumping and an odd moan from the lean-to adjacent to the soddy. Murphy had kept a horse and implements there. One of the masked men whirled away. Another injured man? A prisoner? Toole drove the sheriff thoughts from his mind. He had to be a doctor now, save a life if he could—which he couldn't unless God in his heaven decreed a day of miracles for outlaws. The thumping in the lean-to ceased.

Toole peeled down the man's britches and drawers, baring a pale abdomen and white flesh at the bottom of the man's sternum. This man had lived indoors. An ugly hole pierced the lower left quadrant.

"I have to turn you," Toole said. The man groaned. On the man's backside a larger exit wound leaked bright blood slowly. The bullet had probably missed the left bifurcated aorta, and had probably hit the descending colon.

"How'd this happen?" Toole asked the injured man.

"Don't talk, Con," A Harvest Queen said.

A name. Toole remembered it. He couldn't disentangle his sheriffing from his doctoring. "I'll sew this up if I can. It'll hurt. I'll give you laudanum later—maybe. Not now."

"Am I going to live? Please be honest with me."

Please. Another polite one, all right. "You might. It missed the vital organs. Pierced intestine, no doubt."

It wouldn't be easy to suture a hole the size of a silver dollar. He dug into his kit for a curved surgical needle and silk floss and a bottle of carbolic. The man screamed when Toole swabbed the area, and groaned under every stitch. Toole drew the flesh together ruthlessly while the man thrashed. Someone held the patient down and the work went

faster. Done at last, Toole slapped an adhesive plaster over
the ugly wound.

"Shall I turn him over now?" A Harvest Queen asked.

"Yes," Toole said.

He extracted a small India rubber tube and worked it into
the entry wound while the man writhed under him.

"This'll drain him. His belly's going to fill with fluids,"
Toole said. "He needs surgery on that intestine."

He cleaned the whole area and slapped on another plaster,
anchoring the tube. That was all he could do except relieve
the man's pain.

"You're lucky so far," he told the man lying on the filthy
clay floor. Some sense of mercy and pity in him kept him
from uttering the barbs that flooded his mind. "But you may
not stay lucky if peritonitis sets in. We'll know in a few days.
Your best hope is to come in with me. I can offer you bed
rest. Surgery. You'll need fluids. But no food. I can lower
your fevers and maybe get you past it."

Con's gaze flicked to his colleagues. "I can't," he said.

Chapter 2

An important datum about Ingmar Drogovich is that he never got mad. He ascribed his success to the realization early in life that emotions were a waste of energy. He wasn't mad now, even though train robbers had cleaned him out and taken Filomena for insurance. Instead, he surveyed the damage and began calculating ruthlessly, his mind clapping probabilities the way ice tongs grabbed ice. He had no doubt he'd recover every cent if he put his mind to it.

He pushed through the throng milling beside the coaches, ignoring the rain lashing his granite jowls, heading toward the express car. Ahead, the big Baldwin four-six steamed like a teakettle as rainwater spat off its hot boiler. He ignored the shouts and sobs of the rain-drenched drummers and farmers who stood bewildered and penniless, helpless as sheep.

Drogovich knew what he'd find up there, and the knowledge drove him as close to rage as he ever permitted. Dim chevrons of grudging light from the windows of the lantern-lit coaches showed the way, but still he stumbled over the gravel roadbed. A faint lantern glow lit a square of ground beside the express car, and he saw brakemen, their caps shining wet, shoving the mob of passengers away. He bulled through, heading toward the express car door, which hung awkwardly off its trolley. It had been blown in.

"You can't go in there!" a brakeman yelled.

Drogovich ignored the man and pushed toward the yellow light. Rain rivered down the sides of the car. He hoisted

11

himself up the iron steps and peered about, knowing what he'd see.

"You can't come in here," the conductor said.

"I'm Drogovich."

The conductor stared sharply. Drogovich made an impressive sight and he knew it. It wasn't just the kinked brass hair flowing back in waves; it was the long Slavic face and gray eyes and muscular build, and well-cut black suit under his cape. But most of all it was the name. Drogovich. Helena gold king.

The conductor nodded. He held a shotgun in his hand but it was small solace. On the floor, lying in a pool of bright blood that soaked his blue waistcoat and white shirt, was the expressman. Dead. Near him a small revolver lay on the floor. Powder smoke drifted across the carbide lamp. A bullet had struck the skinny man in the chest.

"Not a pretty sight, is it?" the conductor said. "Murder. They stopped at nothing. Killed a fine man, killed a brave man, killed a father—Hodgpeth. Left a widder and two girls and a boy. Deader'n beef. Fought to defend himself; didn't give quarter. I tell you, Drogovich, this world's a sorry place."

Drogovich didn't waste more than a glance. He was looking for something else, knowing what he'd find. Two rolled steel strongboxes had been quietly loaded into this car on a Helena siding before the car was coupled to this Northern Pacific 57 eastbound passenger train. In them were the fruits of the Fate mine: gold bullion worth two hundred thousand dollars. The boxes lay scattered, each expertly blown by someone gifted in the use of small charges. Judging from the lingering odor, Drogovich thought the charge may have been dynamite, the explosive that Swede, Nobel, had cooked up from nitroglycerine and clay. The robbers had used a massive pry bar to bend out the lip of the strongbox cover. A charge had been tamped into the hollow and ignited, all in a matter of seconds. The small twenty-pound ingots had been plucked from the boxes and hauled away.

The entire output of the Fate since he had snatched it. Ten

thousand troy ounces of .999 pure gold. Eight hundred thirty-three troy pounds. About 683 avoirdupois pounds. Hauled off by at least four packhorses because deadweight was hard on an animal.

"They got it, Mr. Drogovich. A professional job if ever I saw one. I never saw the like, and I've been riding rails for like onto two decades. Bloody villains. Oh, they'll pay in hell sometime. God's in his heaven."

Drogovich suppressed his instinct to shut up the paste-faced conductor who was interrupting his thoughts.

"We'll see," he said. He squatted beside the black boxes, sniffing. He picked up the expressman's revolver, a .38 caliber. All six chambers held spent shells. The dead man had obviously been surprised. Given another moment, he would have reached the shotgun now in the hands of the conductor.

"We've got to get this man to a doctor," the conductor said.

"He's dead."

"We should anyway."

"We'll need a sheriff. How far are we from Miles?"

"Maybe four miles. The sheriff there's a doc."

"A doctor? A sheriff who's a doctor?"

"Yessir."

"How'd that happen? He's probably no good at both."

"I hear tell he's good, even if he's Irish. You never know about micks."

"How'd they stop us?"

"The engineer, Hoss Foche, says a man waved him down with a lantern. There's a trestle over a slough ahead. He figured it was a washout. They had a couple of confederates on board too."

Ingmar Drogovich stepped around the blown-in door and peered out into the rain. He saw the dim faces of brakemen, and beyond, in a wet blur, a hushed crowd. *How did they know?* he thought. No one knew he was heading east with the gold. Not even his own people. Not the railroad, not the American Express company. Maybe the crooks didn't know. Maybe it was dumb luck. This had all the earmarks of a professional job. No sooner had the train hissed to a stop than a pair of robbers had burst into the salon at the rear of his Pullman Palace Car, forced him to stand and raise his hands, plucked a small revolver from his breast pocket, relieved him of a few dollars—he never carried much cash; never had to—and then herded Filomena out.

"Don't follow us or she'll get hurt," said one who sported a Pillsbury's Best flour sack over his face.

"Go to hell," Filomena had yelled. She had his brass hair that fell in kinked waves, but not his mental faculties. She was as hot-tempered as he was cold.

Drogovich had nodded. He was studying boots. The robbers wore black hightops. They weren't cowboys. The Younger gang maybe—what was left of it. Or the Daltons.

At the Pullman Palace Car door, Filomena had refused to budge. "I'll get my hair wet," she snapped.

They'd shoved her out. She'd spat.

"I'll get even, just wait," she'd yelled.

That had been the last he'd seen of her. He'd rushed forward into the coach ahead and found robbery in progress. Two more of them had been systematically extracting every last dime from terrified passengers and not missing a trick. They'd gotten a wedding ring a woman had furtively slid into her bosom. They'd gotten a wad of bills a gent had stuffed into his shoe. They'd busted open the door of the necessary room and gotten a pocket watch from a squatter. They'd threatened instant death to all followers and possemen. They'd advised the passengers to forget what any of the bandits looked like or wore.

Dumb luck, Drogovich thought. They couldn't have known about the bullion. They'd come prepared to blow the express company safe—and got lucky. He turned to look at the safe. The gilded black safe remained untouched. The sight of that virgin safe sent doubts crawling through him. Maybe they'd struck at him, Ingmar Drogovich, after all, and all the rest was camouflage. Even the site for the heist, over three hundred miles from Helena, might have been camouflage. *But how could they have known?*

A perfect night for a heist, he thought. A hammering rain like this would dissolve the trail, melt the spoor, dissolve every hoofprint in the liquid gumbo. On the other hand, horses couldn't go far or fast up to their fetlocks in gumbo. And wagons would mire down.

It was one or the other: dumb luck by a gang that had no idea that the train carried a fortune, or else a heist aimed directly at him by someone in Helena—who knew. He didn't know which it was but he knew he'd find out soon enough. The Fate hadn't fallen into his hands easily. He had enemies there. But when he considered who they were, he shrugged, suddenly amused. It was his nature to be amused in a moment like this, when he'd lost two hundred thousand dollars and his daughter had been abducted, and a dead man lay on bloody hardwood flooring a few feet from him.

Probably dumb luck. The possibility that Elwood Attabury III had planned and executed something like that was too preposterous to consider. Not Attabury, the patrician Bostonian geologist and engineer who'd discovered and built the Fate. Drogovich smiled. Not that pompous aristocrat with too many brains. But maybe Attabury'd hired some professionals, the gold king thought. He doubted it. Attabury would be the gentleman to the end, paying vice with virtue. Drogovich's vice.

Another brakeman wielding a hickory brakeman's club pushed through the mob and clambered into the express car.

"My God," he said. The sight of the expressman's body unnerved him. He stared. "Mr. Graves, there's a second-class passenger in the first coach who's been pistol-whipped. Nasty cut on his head. He's seeing double—concussion maybe."

The conductor nodded. "We need a doctor. No sense staying here. Get the passengers inside, please." Graves turned to Drogovich. "We'll back into Miles. You'd best go back to your car, sir."

"I'll stay here."

"It's against regulations—"

"I'm Drogovich."

"I'm Valentine Graves and this is my train."

"That was my gold—and daughter."

The conductor sighed and vanished into the night. Drogovich heard shouting. Heard questions. Heard Graves telling those sheep that the expressman was dead. That they'd back into Miles City. Moments later the whistle shrilled. Drogovich peered out of the express car door and saw the last of the passengers being herded into their steam cars. Ahead, he heard a heavy thump as the engineer threw the Johnson bar into reverse. After another interminable moment of shrilling whistles and swinging brakemen's lanterns, the brass-bound forty-ton behemoth shrieked and belched steam, the piston rods convulsed, and the drive wheels slowly turned backward, banging car into car as the slack left the link pin couplings and the train huffed slowly back toward Miles City. Wood smoke eddied into the open door, driven down by the pelting rain.

Drogovich, alone with the dead expressman, took his time. He studied the express car safe to see if it had been tampered with. It hadn't. He studied the caved-in express door. Its latch had been blown, leaving a ragged hole in splintered hardwood. The robbers hadn't tried to shoot it off; they'd simply wedged a small charge between the loose-hanging door and the wall of the car and fired it, taking a piece of the wall and the lock with them. No wonder the expressman had been surprised. The concussion would have knocked him flat.

Someone who knew explosives had done it. Someone gifted and fast. A mining man maybe. It seemed improbable to him that some routine train robber like the late Jesse James would have had the sort of skill to do this. They'd have shot or pried their way in. The finger pointed back to the Fate Mine—and the ones he'd wrested it from.

He rolled the body over. The man's brown eyes stared blindly toward the grimy roof of the coach. His flesh felt as cold as the potbellied stove at the far end of the express car. Hodgpeth. He'd died bravely. Drogovich respected him. Most of the lackeys would have raised their arms and licked boots. Six shots too. Probably struck one or two of the robbers. If any had been injured, tracking them down would be easier.

He thought at last of Filomena and wondered. She'd probably stab them all with one of her hat pins and waltz out. Or blister them all with her sweet tongue until they ditched her. The thought amused him. Filomena had her mother's temper, but she had his will. Snobby girl. She'd let them know it. She didn't know her old man was a robber too, who used bought judges, shysters, and goon squads. He laughed. Snotnosed girl. He'd get her back. He was semi-fond of her. He'd make sure her abductors never got as far as a trial. There were things to keep quiet at all costs.

Confederates on board, Graves had said. Two probably boarded at Miles City. At least two more jumped the engineer and fireman. Two or three blew the express car door and then the strongboxes. Someone held horses and loaded gold.

The Northern Pacific eastbound chuffed backward as if it had all the time in the world. Railroad rules, he knew. A brakeman with a lantern would be standing on the platform of the Pullman Palace Car, the one named Marquette in gilt letters on its green lacquered side, where lately he and Filomena had sat having a last sherry before retiring to their plush sleeping rooms. They'd been the only first-class passengers.

While the train backed through inky black laced with rain, Drogovich began a list. Elwood Attabury III was at the top, but only because there were no other names. At Miles City he'd wire a certain party in Helena he'd often used for such purposes and begin to deal with this his own way. He needed men. And information. Such as whether the hoity-toity mining engineer was in his home this night.

The Miles City station announced itself with blurry yellow light spilling from a single window. No doubt the telegrapher's office. The train clanked to a halt like a dying snake. Drogovich peered out the express car door, not seeing another light anywhere. He clambered out, feeling the cold lash of rain again. Graves and a brakeman ran toward the station. Drogovich followed.

At the telegrapher's office they burst into a wall of heat. The man had kindled a fire in the black potbelly to drive away the chill.

"Clewes! We've been robbed. Wire up the line," Conductor Graves said.

Clewes set down his *Police Gazette* and approached the shining brass key. "Robbed?" he muttered. "On a night like this?"

"On a night like this," Graves retorted. "And the rain's helping them. A man's murdered. Hodgpeth. American Express. Passenger's injured. Gold shipment lost. Wire Bismarck. Wire Livingston."

Clewes drafted a message on a yellow pad. "Need to see what I'm saying," he muttered. Then his adept fingers began the Morse waltz, tapping dit dit dah, dit dah dit.

"Come with me, Mr. Drogovich. We'll get Toole. He lives five blocks from here." Graves turned to a brakeman. "Have Hoss Foche put it on the siding. There'll be through traffic. Take care of the passengers. Bring the injured man into the station."

"I have some wiring to do," Drogovich replied.

"No you don't. I want that line open. You come with me. You can tell Toole why you shipped gold without telling the railroad or letting us post special guards. How much was it, by the way?"

Drogovich didn't like being grilled by Graves. They all got that way, absolute lords over their trains and everything on them. "Not much. Private financial information, Graves."

"Come along, sir," Graves demanded.

Drogovich followed, a certain respect building in him for the thin conductor with the bristling mustache and a nononsense way. The conductor lit the way with his brakeman's lantern, throwing a bobbing island of light around them.

They passed looming dark structures, two of which had red lanterns glowing.

"Sporting district," Graves said. "This is Sixth Street. Toole lives over on Eighth and Pleasant."

"Looks like most of the ladies have shut down for the night," Drogovich said. "We run two twelve-hour shifts at our mines. That's how to do business."

"Rain," the conductor said.

They reached a cross street faintly lit by lamps in saloon windows, pale light glittering in the puddles and quagmire. Drogovich lumbered through muck and manure, not minding this rainy-night tour of Miles City, Montana Territory.

"Main Street. The main stem," Graves said. "Toole'll have a posse out in an hour or two. He'll need help. Need to treat the injured man. One thing, sir. Those infernal murderers won't get far. Not on a night like this."

"Maybe I'll go with the posse."

Graves eyed him sharply. "You're not—"

"Drogovich's gold," Drogovich said in a way that ended questioning. And my daughter, he thought. He fully expected her to capture them all and run them in. Her blistering tongue would serve better than a shotgun. The young lady needed a man. Drogovich knew all the signs. She was nearing spinsterhood and scared off every suitor in sight.

They plunged up a street unlit by any lamp and finally swung into a lot with a small calcimined cottage on it.

"Toole's house. Surgery in front," Graves explained.

Not much of a house, Drogovich thought. No wonder the mick doctor needed two jobs.

Graves banged the knocker hard, making it sound like an artillery barrage. The house sighed softly in the rain. He rattled the knocker again. "Toole!" he roared. An amazing amount of voice was erupting from the man's bobbing Adam's apple.

No one answered.

"Sleeping hard. They always sleep hard early in the night. We'll bang on a rear window," Graves said.

The conductor plunged around the side, rapping glass until it shivered and protested. "Toole!" he roared.

The cottage lay silent.

"Maybe he's gone somewhere," Graves said, plunging to the rear. He opened the door of the carriage barn, with Drogovich following. A saddler and a carriage dray stared at them from their stalls, their eyes glassy.

"Huh," Conductor Graves muttered. "Maybe he's patrolling the saloons. If you want an Irishman, head for a saloon."

"Maybe something's wrong here," Drogovich said.

"On a rainy night? There's no crime on a rainy night, Mr. Drogovich."

They both laughed. But a faint irritation was building in the gold tycoon. With every passing minute the robber gang was adding distance.

That's when Drogovich thought he heard a faint thump from within the cottage.

"You hear something?" he asked.

The conductor nodded. Wordlessly they tried the front door, found it unbolted, and entered. They heard the thumping again.

"Toole?" he yelled.

The reply was another thump.

Chapter 3

Elwood Attabury III grieved. In spite of all their planning—their *genius*—things hadn't gone well. Constantine had taken a bullet and might die of it. A brave and honorable expressman lay dead. They hadn't intended to kill anyone. It choked him to think about it. Con Luce had fired the fatal shot; and the expressman had shot Luce. A certain bitterness engulfed Attabury: Drogovich had opened a wound that bled and bled. The expressman hadn't been the first to suffer because of Drogovich's greed.

Toole stood up. "I have to take him in. His life depends on it. His stomach'll fill with fluids, infect—"

"No," said Attabury from under his flour-sack mask.

"I might be able to save him. Abdominal surgery. Cold compresses to keep his fever down when the peritonitis starts. Without that"—he glanced at the sweating gray-fleshed man on the ground—"I don't think he has much chance."

"No."

"May I ask why not?"

"No."

Attabury knew he couldn't let Constantine Luce go. Drogovich would instantly recognize the former superintendent of the Fate Mine. And when that happened, every man among them would be fingered. The knowledge tore at him. He had to let Con Luce die—to save the rest, including himself.

Toole looked tired and defeated. "Is it because I'm the sheriff? You've caused some kind of trouble, A Harvest Queen. I'll hear the rest of it when I get back to Miles."

There was a question in his face. Attabury understood. Toole was wondering if he'd ever see Miles City again.

Attabury didn't reply. He was seriously considering taking Toole with him. Two prisoners. Toole to doctor Luce; the girl for insurance. It might be better to have the sheriff with him than chasing him. He studied his men as they waited in the dim light of the soddy. They all wore flour sacks or bandannas; Toole would have little to go on.

"Con," he said, "can you travel?" Too late, he realized he'd used a name.

Con shook his head. "Hurts too much. Oh, God, it hurts. Just leave me." He lay groaning. Toole knew the pain alone could throw the man into shock. His perforated colon was pouring poisons into the man's gut. The wounds were torturing him.

"Can't do that," Attabury said. "You know why." The silence thickened. Attabury knew it was up to him. He'd put this whole thing together. "Dr. Toole, have you laudanum?"

Toole didn't reply. Attabury squatted, dug into Toole's Gladstone, found the compartment with materia medica in bottles and cartons. He looked for a familiar blue rectangular bottle and found it. Tincture of opium, said the handwritten label. He plucked it up and found it was nearly full. Relief flooded him. The bottle was Luce's ticket out of here. And Toole's ticket too, though Toole didn't know that.

"Laudanum," he said to Con Luce. He squeezed out six drops—a heavy dose—directly into Luce's mouth. The wounded man licked his lips. They waited. It didn't take long. Luce's breathing changed. His gasping vanished. "All right," he said.

"That's seven dollars for the house call and four for the laudanam," Toole said, a faint mockery in his eyes.

Attabury wondered if the man was serious.

"And you're all under arrest," Toole added. "Just for the record. Surrender now and come in. It'll go easier for you than resisting an officer of the law. Turn me down and you'll add another crime—to whatever you've done."

Crime. The word struck at the heart of Elwood Attabury III. Toole was smiling faintly.

"If you can't pay now, pay later. I'll put it on my books. In whose name shall I carry the account? Eh?"

By God, thought Attabury, Toole was having his fun.

"Enough," Attabury said. He rummaged in Toole's bag and helped himself to more plasters, some bandaging, and the bottle of carbolic. Then he snapped the bag shut and handed it to Toole.

"Medical supplies. Two dollars," Toole said. "Where shall I send the statement?"

Attabury ignored him. "Let's go," he said. "Toole, you can walk back after we leave." Then he remembered the girl in the lean-to shed. "No. Wait. Toole, I'm taking you partway back." He turned to the rest. "Ten minutes."

"I'll send the bill east. To Boston," Toole said.

A good guess. Attabury ignored him. Sheriff Toole had his ways.

"How about Philadelphia? I'm not quite familiar with all these Yankee dialects."

"Out," yelled Attabury, keeping some distance between Toole and himself. Some instinct warned him that mild Dr. Toole could turn into a dangerous lawman.

"Harvard," Toole said.

"Shut up."

Outside, the cold rain lashed into them, instantly soaking his flour-sack mask again. He motioned for Toole to get onto a bay. No sense blindfolding him if the sheriff knew where he was. "Ride ahead of me. I'll tell you which way to go."

"To the bluffs," said Toole. "All the world's a bluff."

They had no lantern, but Attabury knew the way. He'd been over this trail before. The horses slopped through a night so black he could barely see Toole ahead.

"What did you do?" Toole asked. "Rob the bank?"

Attabury didn't answer.

"You're too polite. A gentleman bandit. What's your degree in? Pedagogy? A teacher maybe. Instruct me. Tell me

the difference between *can* and *may*. If you use *may* you're
seeking permission, aren't you?''

Attabury felt naked. Why had he supposed he and his men
could pull it off? He knew why he'd done it: because Drogovich owned the politicians and judges, the coppers and the
lawyers; the footpads and the streets. There'd be no justice
in Last Chance Gulch. Not as long as Ingmar Drogovich
ruled Lewis and Clark County. Not as long as Drogovich's
goons patrolled the streets; his captains and spies bought
information from every barkeep; his hundred dollar bills pur-
chased mayhem, incited the press to libel, made court records vanish, tilted the scales of blind justice. Attabury knew
exactly why he and his loyal friends had done it. But he didn't
know how hard it'd be or how easily he'd be spotted for an
amateur.

''I'm Santiago Toole. And you are . . . ?''

''I'm—'' Attabury caught himself. This doctor and sheriff
alarmed him with tricks winging out of the black. ''Toole.
One more word and your skull'll hurt for a month.''

''You can't see to hit me,'' Toole said.

''I can see to shoot. There's a three-quarter moon above
those clouds.''

''I don't think you're capable of it,'' Toole replied. ''In
fact—''

Toole suddenly spurred the horse. It skidded, hooves flail-
ing in mud, and finally burst forward in a spray of muck.

''Stop!'' Attabury yelled. He grabbed for his revolver,
feeling its cold wet grip fill his hand, and lifted it. And didn't
pull the trigger. Toole vanished into the gloom. Attabury dug
heels into his horse and pursued, guided only by the rhythmic
splashing ahead. He wanted that horse. He needed to put
Toole afoot at least a half hour from Miles City. Getaway
time.

But horseback riding hadn't been included in his engineering curriculum. He rode clumsily, his chestnut gelding
skidding and lunging. Toole gained ground.

''Stop!'' Attabury yelled. He shot into the air, unwilling
to aim at the invisible but noisy target swiftly pulling ahead.

The noise didn't stop. Attabury fired again, but Toole didn't even slow down.

Lost him. And that horse would cut down the time it took for Toole to get back to Miles, wire for help, and put a posse together. He reined his wet horse up, feeling the fool again. Dr. Toole was Sheriff Toole, and Sheriff Toole had pegged his man. Chagrined, Attabury turned the chestnut back toward the soddy. They had to run. And take advantage of the hard rain.

Minutes later he found the soddy, a bleary light leaking from its open door. They were all waiting inside, including Her Majesty Filomena.

"Well, was he right? Harvard?" she asked. "You look like one. I prefer men."

She'd been doing that ever since they'd taken her, and no one could shut her up.

"Gag her," he said.

"My tongue's too honest for you?"

"No. We don't want you giving us away."

"You'll give yourself away. That doctor got half of what he needed to know for free."

That was the last she said. Astleheim, his big, square, black-haired sapper, slapped a bandanna over her mouth, cutting off her next sally like a slice of sausage. She lashed at him, scratching his blue-bearded jowl. He pinned her hands and tied her wrists behind her. She yelled something obviously obscene into her gag. Attabury poked his fingers in his ears. The air was less blue with Filomena Drogovich gagged.

Astleheim hoisted her onto a wet horse as if she were a powder keg. But her fuse was wet, and she slumped glumly in her saddle.

They helped Constantine Luce up. He had no trouble at all, and plainly felt no pain either. He clutched the blue bottle fiercely, and then slid it into a breast pocket.

"Magic," he said. "I can stand this trip."

The rest led the packhorses out from the shed. Each was burdened by custom-made small panniers of tough leather, capable of standing up under the shifting weight of gold bullion.

He steered them into a coulee and down a long grade in the middle of a roiling torrent of water that washed away signs of their passage as fast as they moved. It would take them to the Tongue River, which would take them back to Miles City.

On the floor before them lay a naked woman. Her hands were bound behind her back; her mouth had been gagged and her ankles bound also. She'd thumped the floor with her feet to summon them.

Ingmar Drogovich admired her tall, lithe form and amber flesh for an instant, even as Conductor Graves pulled a coverlet from the bed and threw it over her.

"Forgive us, madam," he said gallantly. "I'll cut you loose and we'll retire."

He extracted a penknife from the pocket of his blue uniform, and cut her gag loose. She coughed as the cloth fell free. Next he drew the coverlet back gently and freed her wrists, and finally her ankles.

"Please wait for me in the surgery," she said, her voice close to tears.

"We've no time," Drogovich said. "Where is he?"

She didn't respond. Graves glared at him. Irritated, he followed Graves out to the doctor's offices. Or was it the sheriff's offices? The confusion built a scorn in him. The town needed a proper sheriff, not some fool of a doctor playing lawman.

Graves found a lamp in the office and lit it with a lucifer from his commodious pockets. Amber light lit a row of green canisters, carboys, a human skeleton wired together with brass, a rocking chair, various wicked-looking surgical tools, a rolltop desk buried under debris, including handcuffs and a stack of dodgers on wanted men.

The woman was certainly taking her time, he thought. She could have slipped on a wrapper. When she appeared at last she was fully clothed. Not just in her dress, but in her hightop shoes, and with a blue blanket cape over her as well, layer upon layer, until only her coppery face and hands remained visible. She had heavy cheekbones and straight black Indian hair, but her eyes were those of a white.

"Where is he?" Drogovich asked.

She eyed him hesitantly, and then Graves, registering his conductor's uniform and cap.

Graves smiled. "I'm Valentine Graves. I'm so sorry to have found you—in that condition. The eastbound was robbed by gunmen. A man was killed and a large amount of bullion stolen." He gestured toward Drogovich. "His gold. His daughter was abducted."

"Where is he?" Drogovich demanded. Her hesitancy cost them time.

She pressed her lips together and said nothing, a dangerous fire flashing in her eyes before she averted them.

Graves eyed Drogovich. "I think perhaps you should wait at the train, sir."

Drogovich bit off a reply but didn't yield. "Obviously they needed a doctor, madam. Or were they simply kidnapping the sheriff as a hostage?"

"Doctor," she said so quietly that Drogovich could scarcely hear her. She annoyed him.

"How many?"

"Three. With masks. One a red bandanna. Two wore flour sacks with holes in them. They took him. Oh, God, if they hurt him—"

"Where?" Drogovich asked.

She glared at him.

"Did they say anything?" he persisted. He wanted information, but she wasn't offering it.

She simply stopped talking.

The conductor eyed him sharply. "Come along, Mr. Drogovich. The sheriff isn't here."

"He's out doctoring robbers and kidnappers." Drogovich turned to her. "Why did he go? He could have refused. He had no business doctoring a bunch of robbers."

She sighed.

"Is there a deputy?" he persisted. "We need a posse."

"No. A town constable."

"Lotta good that'll do," Drogovich said.

"Santiago Toole will help any wounded man—no matter who he is. Even an Indian," she said softly.

"That's what's wrong with him," Drogovich replied. "Idealists are fools. They ruin everything. Well, Drogovich'll have to do this himself. Let's go, Graves. I've some wires to send and men to hire. And the N.P.'s going to help. Drogovich's out two hundred thousand dollars."

Graves ignored him. "Are you all right, Mrs. Toole?" he asked.

"My husband was taken away at gunpoint."

"I'll send someone over to keep watch with you."

She stared. "I'll manage," she whispered.

"I think I'd better send someone. You're in danger. You witnessed a crime. And he's the sheriff, after all. If they abduct you—"

"Thank you for freeing me." She averted her eyes.

Drogovich smiled. Freeing her was the best part of it. Graves had been too gallant too fast. "I don't have time for this," he said, pushing into the rain.

Graves followed with the lantern.

"Stupid doctor," Drogovich said as they trotted back toward the station through a stinging deluge. "All he had to do was say no. What could they do? Shoot him? What would it profit them? One dead doctor no longer able to help out. Irish are too sentimental."

"You don't know that, sir. They might have shot him on the spot—or threatened his wife. How'd you like to have desperadoes threaten your wife with death—or worse?"

"Drogovich would have paid them good money to do it," he retorted, thinking of his estranged fat Elsa, living in Teaneck, New Jersey.

"I've talked with Toole many a time. He often meets the trains. He's esteemed here—good sheriff and good doctor. He surprises people. Don't underestimate him, sir."

Drogovich didn't like lectures. Make some yokel a con-

ductor and it went to his head. "This Sheriff Toole, this Dr.
Toole, wasn't here when I needed him. He could have been.
Any good sheriff would have been. I don't forget. Ingmar
Drogovich never forgets. And never forgives."

Graves said nothing as they trotted down Sixth Street
again. One last red lamp burned. Ahead of them on Pacific
Avenue the station glowed from every window, and the
coaches of the eastbound spilled light.

Wild frustration boiled through Drogovich. He wanted a
posse; armed power, gathered swiftly, led by a proper lawman, out in the night tracking down bandits. He personally
would shoot them all. Save a trial! The thought bothered
him. He'd actually never taken a life. Emotions were always
the weakness. It had been a cardinal rule of his life, and one
of the keys to his success, that he never succumbed to his
feelings.

Now that he thought about it, he didn't want a posse. He
wanted a few hired men of a special sort who'd do as directed
and ask no questions. He might even find them in the saloons, late as it was. But he doubted it. Better to wire Helena
and have his own men shipped down on a special, horses
and all. He'd make a posse, all right. His own. With several
gents he'd employed for years, gents with certain skills and
certain attitudes. Highball a special here and they'd be ready
to ride by mid-morning. Toole or no Toole. Law or no law.

He strode swiftly along the station platform, heading for
the telegraph office, when an apparition blossomed in the
darkness. A man wearing a black slicker, riding a soaked
horse, hastened toward the station at a trot.

"Why—that's Toole!" Graves said.

Drogovich stopped suddenly. He beheld a slim, black-
haired man who looked too young to be either sheriff or
doctor. Was this man Miles City's excuse for the law?

"We've been robbed. Where've you been?" he demanded.

Toole dismounted slowly, lifting a black Gladstone bag as
he slid lightly off the horse. "I know," he said. "And who
are you?"

"That's my daughter they took. Did you treat her?"

Toole stared. "I'll be with you in a moment. My wife's in trouble."

"We found her. I . . . freed her. She's upset," Graves said.

Toole's glare bored into the conductor, who met it unflinchingly. Then briefly he surveyed Drogovich.

"I'll go to her. She'll want to know." He clambered back onto his wet horse.

"Sheriff. She's all right. You'll go after that gang, and right now."

Toole turned. "Who did you say you were?"

"Drogovich."

The name didn't register with the man. "Well, Mr. Drogovich, I'll be back in a few minutes."

"We've an injured man. Hit on the head with the barrel of a revolver. And a dead man," Graves said.

Toole sighed and slid off the horse. "Let's see the injured one," he said. "I may have to go to my house anyway. For supplies."

The conductor led Toole into the station, where the injured passenger lay across a brown-enameled waiting room bench. A vicious gash had leaked blood into the hair over his right ear. He looked pale and kept his eyes shut.

Toole slid out of his slicker and knelt beside the man, studying the wound and the large lump on the man's head. "I'm a doctor," he said, sliding his hand into the work-hardened left one of the man. "Open your eyes. Can you see me?"

The man's eyes flickered open and shut, as if lamplight had blinded him. "Sort of," the man muttered. "Double. Everything's double."

Time was wasting. Drogovich wheeled toward the telegraph office.

"Mr. Drogovich," Toole yelled. "Where are you going?"

"Getting help."

"Just hold your bloomin'· horses. I'll be with you directly."

But Ingmar Drogovich didn't stop, and no two-bit sheriff would stop him. He plunged in, composing a coded message even as he waited impatiently for Clewes to transcribe the messages clicking and clacking in on a line that pulsed with life in the night.

Soon he'd have his private army.

Chapter 4

When they reached the valley of the Tongue, Elwood Attabury led them out upon a riverside trace that would take them straight toward Miles City. They followed silently, none of them enjoying the rain rivering down their slickers. They numbered six men plus Filomena Drogovich. Con Luce, the erstwhile superintendent of the Fate, hung weakly to the saddle horn, buoyed along in painless limbo by the laudanum. The man's life-or-death struggle with peritonitis lay ahead. Beside him rode Karl Astleheim, the former foreman at the mine and a pyrotechnic genius who had shaped the special charge they'd wedged between the express car wall and the suspended loose-fitting door. Moments later he'd blown the strongboxes open as well, after prying pockets in cold steel. He had good reason to hate Drogovich.

Among them was a Welsh hard-rock miner, a mucker nicknamed Chico for no fathomable reason. He had the build of an ox, perhaps because he'd spent most of his life shoveling rock into ore cars. Chico knew pack animals, and had taken care of the mine's mules, and now was leading the gold-laden packhorses on a picket line behind him.

At the rear, guarding Filomena, rode two more men who had good reason to despise Drogovich. Enrico Ferrero had been a driller in the Fate. He could wield a mean sledgehammer but had scarcely ever ridden a horse. The other half of that odd couple was Angus Dillingham, the Fate's young and consumptive bookkeeper—who had refused to be bribed by the minions of Ingmar Drogovich. The flame of righteousness burned hot in him.

A less probable gang of train robbers had never been assembled, Attabury thought. But not a one of them imagined they were engaging in anything felonious—at least not until things fell apart; an expressman had died at Luce's hand; a rebellious passenger had been pistol whipped by Ferrero—and Luce rode the knife edge of death. Now, as they fled down the river, the sobering reality settled on all of them, especially Elwood Attabury III, young Bostonian with a degree in geology and engineering. Attabury had been in the first graduating class of the new Massachusetts Institute of Technology, where he'd switched after two languorous years at Harvard; a mining genius who could track down high-grade ore better than anyone alive. He'd discovered the lode that became the Fate—only to see it stolen.

Their evil fate lay heavily on him now. A brave and innocent expressman dead. Luce . . . But there was no help for it. If God was in his heaven, he'd smile upon this desperate act of robbing a robber of his spoils. At least that is what Attabury told himself as he plowed through walls of cold water. The rain had been a blessing, washing away every trace of their passage. Maybe the hand of God. Drogovich owed more: this booty didn't begin to pay the man's debt. Each of the six would receive some small fraction of the ruin Drogovich had imposed on him, and Attabury would get the smallest percentage of all. But that was fine: Chico, Ferrero, and Dillingham needed it more.

Tree branches slapped his face, and he realized suddenly he'd strayed from the trace. He stopped, trying to find his bearings, letting his senses lead him.

"Left," Luce said.

The man's painless peace disturbed Attabury, whose puritan streak insisted that a wounded man ought to suffer.

Attabury turned left and felt the horse step into a rocky trough he took to be the trace. Thus they fumbled forward until a faint yellow glow ahead announced the presence of Milestown—Miles City, the boosters were calling it now. He

paused at the railroad bridge across the Tongue. The bright-
lit station stood less than half a mile to the east. A train stood
on a siding there, and Attabury surmised it was the one they'd
stopped.

They had to cross the Tongue. Attabury worried about the
rain-swollen river but steered them into it and over a soft
bottom to its west bank. A short time later they reached the
military bridge. At that point some of the buildings of Miles
City lay only a few yards away. After studying the blackness,
seeking observers and finding none, he led them under the
bridge along a dry flat. Filomena yelled. She'd worked her
gag loose. Someone back there shut her up.

When they approached the confluence of the Tongue and
the Yellowstone, Attabury turned west and they passed directly under the beetling brow of Fort Keogh. He pushed
onward toward a place they had studied in advance. Up the
Yellowstone a few miles lay a crudely made rowboat used by
local ranches. It rested on its gunnels, overturned, a pair of
oars tucked underneath. A clear animal trail suggested a ford
there, or at least a spot where livestock had to swim only
briefly.

He let his horse pick its way up the river bottoms for what
he judged to be a half hour. But he didn't see the rowboat;
indeed, he scarcely saw anything. It had seemed so simple
when they'd surveyed all this by daylight: the boat lay a half
hour upriver from Keogh. There'd be a bright moon the night
of the heist, and they would find the boat easily. They hadn't
counted on clouds so thick they blotted out almost all light.

"You think we've passed it, Con?"

"I don't know. Are we a half hour west of the post?" The
man was breathing hard and had slumped in the saddle.

"I don't know. Too dark to read the hands. Best keep
going, I guess."

He found nothing. He rode another fifteen minutes while
the rest dutifully followed. Dread engulfed him. He'd missed
the rowboat. The darkness hid it and would keep on hiding
it even if they retraced their route.

"What do you think?" he asked.

"Let's keep on going and look for another ford," Dillingham said.

"Take me back before I catch pneumonia," Filomena said. "And before you catch something worse."

Attabury ignored her. He'd never met her but he knew all about her. Everyone in Helena knew all about her.

"Not much chance of fording when the river's so high," Luce said.

"Hi go back und hlook. Hi got night eyes," Astleheim said.

"All right. We'll wait."

Astleheim turned his livery stable plug and vanished. Attabury wondered if he'd ever see the sapper again. The man steered toward the gurgling water, intending to stick to the bank.

"Who can I bribe?" Filomena said. "How about you?" She addressed Ferrero. "A dollar?"

Ferrero muttered.

"Or are you worth five? Probably not. My father buys your sort for a dollar a day."

Ferrero grunted.

Filomena turned to Attabury. "Well? What about you? You speak English at least. Set me free and I'll donate fifty cents. You can name the charity."

"You're coming along."

"Well thanks. I'm honored. I'm also in need. Are you going to see me to the bushes?"

It embarrassed Attabury. She could slide away and never be found in this sort of blackness. "You can get off. You can't walk. No one'll see you anyway."

"I'll wait," she replied. "You're so gallant."

Attabury ignored her. Gossip had it that Filomena's tongue had withered the courage of every young suitor she'd encountered. She would anger him too, if she found the smallest chink in his armor.

"I suppose you'll all have your way with me," she said.

He wanted to say no, no no; some instinct told him to remain absolutely silent.

"I think I would enjoy it. In the dark they all look alike."

She grated on Attabury's puritan instincts.

She stopped as suddenly as she'd started, and they waited again. But not long. The crash of a horse mauling brush reached them and Astleheim loomed up.

"Yah," he muttered.

They followed him, banging through riverbank brush, until at last they bumped into the boat. Attabury rejoiced. The powder man had rescued them. Swiftly they righted the rowboat and loaded in the heavy packs of gold and their pack of supplies. Chico and Ferrero got in and rowed toward the north bank, losing ground to the current. On the far shore the pair unloaded, and then Chico rowed back alone. Astleheim ferried Filomena, Luce, and Dillingham over while Chico tied the unburdened horses to a long picket line and then rode into the watery void himself, tugging them along. The horses rebelled at water's edge, and Attabury had to whip them in.

Attabury could see Chico and the horses only for the first few yards, and then the gloom swallowed them. He dreaded the possibility that Chico and the horses would simply be swept away by the swift current. That they'd be lost. He waited tensely on the south bank for what seemed forever, and then Chico and his saddle horse splashed into sight. They tied the second group of horses to a picket line and Chico crossed again, and again Attabury worried.

Slowly they got everyone across. On the far shore they were able to account for everything. Nothing lost. But there was still one thing more to do: Chico would row the boat back, swimming his horse. He would overturn the rowboat and slide the oars under it, and swim his weary horse northward one last time. They had to leave the boat where it had been—or give themselves away. Chico vanished into the gloom once again, while Attabury loaded the gold and supplies on the packhorses, put Filomena on her plug, and made ready to travel.

Con Luce slid the blue bottle from his pocket and took more than a nip.

Elwood Attabury decided to say something to his dispirited men while they waited. "We've had some setbacks," he said. "It hurts to think about them. We pray God for your health, Con. We grieve the loss of that expressman. We didn't want that." He paused, peering at blurred forms in the intense gloom. "But we're here. We succeeded. We paid old Drogovich in kind. We'll go on. Be proud of what you've done. You've done well, and no man failed. We each did what he had to. We'll see what we have in those panniers when the sun shines. It won't be enough. Nothing we took tonight will equal what that bandit took from us in wealth, in happiness, in sickness and injury."

Too late he remembered Filomena there, blotting up his words. Now she knew. And he couldn't let her go.

So much to do. Santiago comforted the injured man on the waiting room bench as best he could. He knew how the man felt. The lowest voice sounded like the clash of cymbals; the gentlest lamplight fried his brain like lightning.

"Is it gonna hurt like this long?"

"Not for long. It's a mild concussion. I think you'd better stay here a few days though. Hotel here. I'll have your bags taken off. You'll need a room."

The man nodded.

Toole stood, trying to sort out priorities. He spotted the conductor and brakemen and thought to put them to work. Not a single resident of Miles City had braved the downpour in the middle of the night to see why a passenger train was halted at the bright-lit station. Toole was entirely on his own.

"Mr. Graves, I need your assistance. The faster we do this, the sooner you can be on your way. I'd like you to brave that rain again. First to my house to let Mrs. Toole know I'm safe. And second to our mortician, Sylvane Tobias. He's a cabinetmaker; his shop's on Eighth and Main; he lives at the rear."

"Very well. How long will this take, sir?"

"I'll need statements from the passengers. A list of valuables."

"I'll have the brakemen start it. There's paper and pencils in Clewes's lair."

"That'd be fine. I'll need their statements and those of the fireman and engineer. Some of those passengers won't be able to write. Find a volunteer to take down their statements. I want every detail. A complete description of each robber. Clothing, size, everything. And what was taken. I want them signed. Name and address so stolen goods can be returned."

The conductor nodded.

Toole chose to play coroner next; a task that fell to him often enough as the combined sheriff and doctor at Miles City.

"Which of your brakemen can identify the expressman? Who found him first?"

"That'd be Philo Hart." He pointed.

Toole pushed toward the stationmaster's office and telegraph room.

"How long'll we be stuck here?" a drummer asked.

"As short as possible," Toole replied.

"Outrageous service."

Toole found Drogovich standing there while Clewes tapped out a message on the brass instrument.

"Clewes. Finish that and send an all-points—"

"I'm busy."

"Wait your turn, Sheriff." Drogovich's tone made it an order.

Toole fought down a temper. "If you impede me in my duties, you'll be in trouble."

"You can wait," Drogovich said.

Clewes signed off and peered up. Toole took the opportunity. "All right, Fortney. You compose it. To sheriffs at all points. N.P. Eastbound Fifty-seven robbed east of Miles at about ten-fifteen. At least six men escaped on horseback with a female hostage. Several packhorses carrying gold bullion and valuables. Wanted for murder and robbery. More coming. Sign me."

"Mr. Drogovich wants me to hold the line open—"

"Send it. Or deal with me later." Toole stared the man down. "Come with me, Mr. Drogovich. I have business in the express car and I want to hear your story while I work."

"I'll stay here, Toole. I'm expecting confidential information."

Toole paused. "Mr. Drogovich. You're impeding the investigation of robbery and murder. I don't happen to care who you are; you'll cooperate or face the consequences."

Drogovich smiled slowly, some odd fires dancing in his eyes. He'd been fashioned from great slabs of muscle that hung in long planes, giving him an aura of barely subdued violence.

"Clewes. What comes in is confidential," he said, and followed Toole. They trotted into the blistering rain, leapt over the mainline rails to the siding, and clambered, half soaked, into the icy express car. A carbide lamp in a wall sconce cast grudging gray light on the scene.

The expressman's body lay on the hardwood floor to the left, the man's open eyes staring at the grimy ceiling. The presence of death subdued them both.

"What's so confidential?" Toole asked, catching Drogovich off guard.

"Why—" Drogovich had to pull his gaze away from the dead expressman. "Toole, you're a card."

"You'd better tell me. It'll be noted in the records."

Drogovich smiled slowly. "Drogovich is starting his own investigation. He has means. He'll get Filomena and the gold back. And a lot faster than—let's say a small-town sheriff."

"Behind my back. We'll discuss that later. Tell me how it happened, and don't miss a trick."

Toole knelt beside the body and lifted a hand, wishing he'd come earlier. Sometimes dead men weren't. But the expressman's hand was stone cold; the man's limb had started to stiffen.

"I'm listening," Toole said.

Cause of death was a bullet wound squarely into the sternum, and, behind it, the heart. The entry wound had not bled much. Toole undid the man's uniform-blue waistcoat, and undid his white shirt. The wound was typical of one made at close range by a large-caliber revolver.

He turned the body over. It resisted, clinging to the floor. He found no exit wound. He wrestled the man's waistcoat up, tugged at his shirt, and found nothing. Unsatisfied, he pulled off the waistcoat entirely, and then the shirt, until the expressman's bluish flesh lay naked in the light.

"Must have been a dud," Drogovich said.

"It hit the sternum—breastbone—and broke it," Toole replied. "May have shattered the ball. I'm waiting, Drogovich. Tell me your story."

"You can wait. Dead men silence me."

Toole saw no need for an autopsy. He dug into the man's pants pockets and found loose change and a dollar bill, along with a skeleton key and a ring of keys. He found the expressman's blue suit coat hanging from a wall rack and probed its pockets, finding a pad of express company freight forms and a pencil. The coat was well-worn, shiny at the elbows and sleeves, grimy about the neck.

The lamplight revealed two splintered white pocks in the enameled green walls; two shots that had missed the expressman. He'd dig out the lead if he could.

Toole turned his attention to two rolled steel strongboxes that had been blown open somehow.

"These yours, Drogovich?"

"They are."

"They held the bullion?"

"Yes."

"How much?"

"That's proprietary information."

Toole turned toward the man. "How much?"

"Too much."

"I have six cells and none of them are comfortable. It's a cold stone jail."

Drogovich looked amused. "About two hundred thousand worth. In bars of twenty troy pounds."

"You're a man of parts. Perhaps you can tell me how those

strongboxes were blown open. It took them only a few seconds. How that car door was blown in, right off its trolley, the lock included. Perhaps you noticed when we entered the car that the door has no bullet holes in it. No one shot out the lock.''

"Someone knew explosives.''

"Who might that be? Have you enemies?''

"A man acquires them.''

"Who knew about this shipment?''

"No one.''

Toole was annoyed. "What did they weigh, loaded?''

"Keep your nose out, Toole. If this was an inside job, Drogovich'll deal with it.''

"It took several men and a dolly to load those boxes into this car. Where were you going with the gold?''

"New York.''

"Who bought your tickets?''

"Drogovich'll deal with that.''

"You're impeding a lawful investigation. I have a cold jail.''

The magnate stood in the middle of the shambles, somehow filling the whole car with his presence like some Dark Ages emperor. "Toole. We'll take care of this. Tomorrow morning a special'll pull in here with some trusted men. We'll do our own hunt. You keep your nose clean and go back to pill-pushing.''

"When?''

"They've probably left Helena by now. Fast as they could get steam up, couple on a coach and boxcar, and put my people on.''

Toole drew himself up, finding himself dwarfed by the blocky magnate. "There'll be no vigilantes running loose in my county, Drogovich.''

"You could deputize them.''

"I deputize men whose character I know.''

Drogovich laughed heartily.

Chapter 5

The brakeman, Philo Hart, clambered in and stopped, his gaze trapped by the corpse.

"Here," Toole said. He draped the expressman's blue suit coat over him. "The dead own the place they rest, don't they? It's hard to talk, hard to think. Even after years as a physician, I don't deal well with it."

The brakeman looked fearfully at the covered body and relaxed slightly. He glanced at Drogovich and then at Toole. "Mr. Graves sent me; said you had questions."

"Tell me what you know, Mr. Hart. From the beginning."

"Why—they flagged us down. I was in the first coach. I heard a thump, a boom sort of. I was about to open the coach door when one of them stuck a gun in my ribs and I couldn't get out. I heard shots, maybe eight or ten, and then more thumps, and I knew we were being took."

"They robbed you and the passengers?"

"They didn't rob me. Just held me. But they told the passengers to ante up and not hide anything because they'd get hurt. One stood at the end of the coach; the other walked down the aisle with a sack, collecting stuff. Then they hit the second coach. I opened the door and tried to see out, but lead was flying."

"Did they rob Graves?"

"You bet. He carries the fare money."

"What did they say?"

"Just warnings. You know. If you wanna live, don't move."

Toole turned to Drogovich. "Were these the same ones? Did they have a sack?"

"Yes. They ran in, waved guns in my face. Took her. Warned me not to follow or she'd be hurt."

"Where was the Pullman porter?"

"Right there at the bar."

Santiago was getting a sense of the event, but had no clues. "What'd you notice about them?"

Hart said, "I was too afraid to notice. I couldn't even give you a description. Big, they were big."

"They wore hightop laced boots," Drogovich said. "And flour sacks. One wore brown corduroy britches. Both wore black kid gloves. One had brown eyes. One was short and stocky. The other skinny and short."

Toole listened. Drogovich was making a point. Lesser mortals like brakemen might be terrified, but not gold magnates. "How'd they talk?"

"What do you mean? They yelled at us."

"Anything unusual in their speech? An accent?"

"Is a robber supposed to talk funny, Toole?"

Santiago kept his counsel. Drogovich would have reacted to polite, educated robbers. Toole didn't feel like sharing information, not when the man had wired for private vigilantes.

"Are you done with me, sir?" Hart asked.

"Not quite. You got here first. What did you see here?"

"Him." Hart nodded at the body. "Dead."

"Dead or dying?"

"He wasn't moving none. All that blood."

"The revolver was about here?" Santiago pointed. "The strongboxes where they are now? The car door blown in like this?"

Hart nodded. "Lots of smoke. I mean, from explosives."

Santiago felt vaguely disappointed and hoped he'd pick up something more useful from the passengers. "All right. Mr. Hart, I'll take these strongboxes as evidence. Would you kindly carry them to the stationmaster's office?"

"I can't lift—"

"There's dollies, I'm sure. And baggage wagons."

"The express company won't like—"

"They belong to Mr. Drogovich here." He waited for Drogovich to muscle him some way or other but the man didn't.

The brakeman clambered out into the rain.

"Hired help get cheeky," Drogovich said.

"So do the Irish. Now I want your story, all of it, and straight. Was this blind luck or was this aimed at you?"

"We've been thinking on it."

"Well, think about this: Withholding information from a law officer investigating a crime might make you an accessory after the fact."

"What's that worth?"

Toole wondered if he was being bribed, and said nothing.

"In hard time. What's it worth?"

Toole spotted a malicious gleam in Drogovich's eye. The gold king was toying with him. He'd toy back. "Withholding information's a two-way street. You get nothing from me."

The man's expression didn't change an iota.

"Very well, Drogovich. There's a hotel across the road, Macqueen House. I'll see you in the morning. I've got to finish this up and let this train go."

Sylvane Tobias appeared at the car door, driving a light wagon with a pine casket on it. And the brakeman arrived with a dolly. Drogovich eyed them and stepped into the wet night.

The cabinetmaker climbed in, eyeing the carnage with a cool eye. "Another white man," he said. "Why can't it be Injuns?"

"Sylvane!"

"Who's paying?"

"His name's Hodgpeth and he left family in Bismarck. I expect American Express'll pay."

"Somebody has to," Tobias said, lifting the blue coat from the dead man's face. "You done with him?"

Toole boiled. "He's a brave man; fought them. Wounded one. That's the trouble with you undertakers—"

"I'm a cabinetmaker. Got stuck with this because no one else—"

"Treat him with respect. He's worthy."

Tobias looked hurt.

"I'm sorry, Sylvane. I'm tired."

"What happened?" Tobias said. Repentance would consist of divulging inside information which Tobias would spend like double eagles in the morning. For Sylvane Tobias, spreading sheriff information like a honeybee was the true wage of undertaking.

"Train robbery," Toole retorted.

Sylvane waited. Toole turned silent. Sylvane looked petulant. "I usually can help you," he said. "Where do you get half your tips?"

The brakeman wrestled one empty strongbox past the body and eased it onto the dolly. Then the second. Toole helped him ease the dolly down to the station platform.

"Making a man get up in the middle of a rainy night," Tobias muttered, staring daggers at Toole.

Toole sighed. "I'll help you with Hodgpeth. I haven't got a first name. Get it from the conductor in there. Graves. Valentine Graves."

"Who was that man in the cape? The one that left when I got here?"

Toole decided to feed a worm to the carp. "Ingmar Drogovich."

"The same one?"

"Sylvane, your logic eludes me."

"The Helena one. They robbed his gold."

Sylvane seemed happy and pulled the lid off the top of the square pauper's box. "I never bring a good box until I know who's paying," he said cheerfully.

"I may need you as a witness. Before we lift him, see where he lies. Look at the wound."

"Fatal. Any others?"

In fact Santiago had failed to look. Cussing himself and wanting to blame his weariness, he swiftly undid the dead man's britches, surveyed a white belly and legs, and shook his head.

"You miss half of it, Toole. I always have to cover your tracks. If it wasn't for me . . ."

They lifted the dead man into the box and Toole clamped the lid down.

"Who did it? How much got took? I suppose old Drogovich's spoiling to go after them."

"Sylvane."

"I always bail you out, and what do I get for it?"

"You're carrying a good man. He's earned your respect and mine. I hope his soul sails right up to God."

"I never believed that stuff, but I do a good imitation at buryings."

"I believe in it all," Toole said. "A mortal is the clay of God. All the saints have gone before me, making the world sweet and straight. That's what's in me."

"I'll bury you next to the Mexicans and behind the Indians," Tobias said. "An Irish papist."

"Get out," Toole snapped. He'd never reconciled himself to the contempt for the Irish he'd found everywhere in this country, and for a moment he felt homesick for Kilkenny.

Tobias clambered into his wagon on the platform and rattled off into the wet night. A terrible weariness overtook Santiago, and he wanted to go home, hold Mimi, crawl into a safe bed. But duty beckoned.

He found Graves in the waiting room. The efficient conductor had gathered statements from all passengers. He handed them to Toole.

"I went over each, Sheriff. Names and addresses. List of properties stolen. Are we free?"

"In a moment. You can tell your fireman to make steam." He turned to the crowd and addressed them all. "Thank you for your cooperation. I'm sorry about the delay. Before you board, can any of you tell me anything that'd help me? Something odd about the robbers? Something they said or did?"

He stared into vacant faces. No one said a thing.

"How are we supposed to get where we're going without

money?'' a man asked. "They took everything I had. I was going to homestead. Me and my missus. Now what?''

Toole shook his head. He had no answer for life's tragedies. "Have you left your name and address and a description of the property with me?''

The man nodded.

"Let's get going," a drummer in a checkered suit yelled. "We've been hung up long enough. You sure took your time.''

Conductor Graves rescued Santiago. He walked slowly to the protester and stared him down. "Be glad it wasn't you in the express car," he said softly. "The N.P. will see you to your destinations. All aboard.''

As he rode through a sodden black, Elwood Attabury III rued the day he'd invented the robbery. It'd all seemed so logical then: Drogovich had stolen the Fate, and owned the streets and courts. There could be no justice other than what Attabury fashioned by his own courage and ability. He'd persuaded the others of the rightness of their course. Until now. So much had gone wrong. The dead and dying and injured. A young woman abducted for no good reason. A lot of hapless passengers robbed of everything just for cover. If they hadn't been robbed, the finger would point squarely at Attabury and his colleagues. He saw them all in his mind's eye, penniless and desperate, lacking even the coin for a meal or bed, or the means to wire for help.

Maybe, he thought, he could contrive to "lose" the booty snatched from innocents. It wouldn't be easy. They'd have to leave it in a place where it'd be "found" by the right people. No. What was done could not be undone. The dead expressman could not, like Lazarus, be restored to life. The bullet hole in Con Luce, reeling in his saddle beside him, could not be removed by some magical incantation.

And so he rode, long thoughts crowding his soul, heaviness and guilt upon him. The fierce rain slackened and then died, and by the time the northeastern horizon glowed an iron-gray, most of the clouds had hurried away. The deluge had started as a friend, washing away their passage. Now it would become their enemy, leaving muddy ground and hoof-prints stamped in the clay like a written confession on an ancient tablet.

They'd climbed the northern bluffs of the Yellowstone valley and headed over a prearranged route that would top a low prairie divide and take them into the valley of the Musselshell River, and west toward Helena across an empty land where their passage would arouse only coyotes. They'd lost their way in the inky dark, but it didn't matter as long as they followed coulees upward and hewed west by northwest. He'd checked his compass now and then, scratching a lucifer to see.

Now, as the predawn light turned his men and horses into pewter, he knew they would have to stop. Con Luce hung on to his saddle horn with a death grip. He might feel no pain under the laudanum, but his strength had vanished. The horses had wearied. The girl was hungry and was announcing her needs loudly. He chose a bench in a wide coulee, hidden from all eyes by the slopes of naked grass and rock. Not a tree or even brush softened the barren country.

"We'll rest here and have coffee," he said.

"Shore we will," Chico said. "Wid all the dry wood for a fire."

Attabury sensed the bitterness in the man. They were all having second thoughts. Every one of them had been an honest citizen before last night. Each of them had suffered and found no hope in Drogovich's courts and judges. He didn't doubt that every one of them now wished it had never happened.

He dismounted and almost collapsed because his legs refused to prop him up. He eased Con Luce down tenderly, and settled him in the wet grass.

"I'm not going to make it," Luce whispered. "It's not the pain—it's the machinery."

"And just where is a lady supposed to go?" Filomena asked.

She had a point. "We'll turn our backs. You dismount and

walk over there." He pointed. "You'll have two minutes. After that we turn around."

Wearily the others complied. They all had sense enough to hold their reins tightly and keep their weapons at hand. He peered at them all, standing there like dead trees, a fortune in their possession but their faces haunted like men who knew they were destined for hell.

"All right," she said. "You should have looked. Enjoyed it. Seeing what you've done to me. You should have laughed. You should do—whatever you feel like. But you aren't men. I wish I'd been taken by real bandits. If you're going to be bad, you should be *bad*. You don't even have the nerve."

She had a point, he thought.

"Amateurs," she added. "Why don't you have your way with me? That'd even the score against my pappy."

Her talk astonished him. She stood there, clearly ascendent, some wild mock in her face, her will and her tongue whipping them even though she was their prisoner.

"I like bad men. Your kind weary me," she added.

He peered at his colleagues. Some of them were trying to muster their manhood in the withering gale. Ferrero smirked. Dillingham the Righteous looked insulted. Astleheim glowered.

"We all feel bad, Miss Drogovich. You're right. We're not robbers. We inflicted harm and it haunts us. We felt we had no choice."

"I want coffee. And breakfast. Will you famish a lady?"

He unbuckled a pannier of their packhorse, dug out hardtack, and handed her several biscuits.

She laughed, and it was the way she laughed that grated on him. It said cruel things without a word being spoken. Some people could turn a laugh into anything, including scorn, which was what underlay her amusement. She bit at it greedily, though.

"I admire the army," he said. "They know how to do things in the field. We worked this out like a campaign. Hardtack is light, doesn't spoil, and keeps a man alive."

"And breaks women's teeth. You'll ruin my looks along

with the rest of me." She clamped her teeth into a biscuit and chewed grimly. The others helped themselves and chewed. He welcomed her silence, knowing it wouldn't last long.

And it didn't. "I'll tattle. I know who you are. You can't release me," she announced, wickedness in her face. "I'll be stuck with you forever. You could marry me. A wife's testimony against her husband doesn't count. Or you could kill me. I forget your name but you owned the Fate before Daddy stole it."

He got the impression she was enjoying herself. And she was. She was simply too strong to be fainthearted now. "Maybe we will," he said. "Do you prefer a bullet or a noose, or should we drown you?" He could banter with the best of them, he thought.

"It'd beat marriage to you," she retorted. "I wouldn't marry anyone who'd lost a high grade gold mine."

Lost wasn't the word, he thought. Drogovich had bought an adjacent claim and announced that the veins apexed on his property. Under mining law, that gave him the right to follow the leads anywhere, to their end. The man had filed suit the same day he'd bought—or rather, stolen—that tiny half acre on the bluff above the Fate. And that'd been only the beginning.

Constantine Luce stared disconsolately at the forbidden food and plucked the blue bottle of joy juice from his breast pocket.

"Easy, Con," Elwood said.

Luce eyed him. "I have a right to die my way," he muttered. "Without the gears squeaking."

"You'll make it. You'll make it! Toole said—"

"I heard what Toole said."

Elwood sighed. "We all need rest," he said to the others. "A few hours."

Chico nodded and began pulling packs off horses. Ferrero helped him with the gold.

"We did the right thing," Angus Dillingham said. "I

wouldn't have done it otherwise. I'm not going to let her—get me down.''

She laughed again, and this time it sounded like a heckler in the back pew. But they ignored her. They picketed the unburdened horses, opened bedrolls over their slickers, and eased into the wet grass and mud. They didn't have a bedroll for her—Elwood's planning hadn't quite compassed every contingency—and he offered her his.

"You should make me lie on the wet ground," she said. "If you treat me badly enough I might keep my mouth shut."

"It's not in me. You're as innocent as those passengers we robbed. I can't do anything for them, but I can do what I can for you."

"Who says I'm innocent?"

"I suppose you sent the plug-uglies to jump my miners. I suppose you bribed the judges and—"

"Oh, he did all that. But I'm no different, you know."

"We agree on something, anyway," he said.

He needed to escape her. Either that or gag her again. He dug into his saddlebag, extracted a brass telescope, and trudged wearily up the steep eastern grade. At its crest the sudden sun riding the misty horizon blinded him.

He settled on the ridge and surveyed a sea of land stretching leagues in every direction, unfenced and scarcely known and certainly not inhabited. It gave him a giddy sense of liberty made all the more painful by the foreboding knowledge that soon Toole would catch up and take it all away. He stretched his brass instrument and peered toward their backtrail, the image bobbing until he steadied it on their hoofprints. He could follow that incriminating trail for almost a mile, he judged, before it blurred to nothing. He saw no one following, but he knew that sooner or later Toole would ride it, and if not Toole, then Drogovich and an army, and if not Drogovich, then that hound Alan Pinkerton, much favored by robbed railroads.

Chapter 6

The rain had stopped, and the first gray hint of a new day rimmed the eastern horizon. Wearily Santiago watched the long-delayed train steam off into the murk. The robbery had eaten up the entire night and his last reserves of energy. The waiting room seemed oddly hollow and forlorn. Even the man with the concussion had gone on after Graves had offered him a Pullman berth gratis. Nothing but the stale odor of tobacco mingled with the subtle scents of fear and anger remained to remind Toole of a night's tragedy.

He ached for sleep, needed to assure Mimi and comfort her, but there were still things to do. He made for the malodorous inner sanctum of the station, where the night telegrapher, Clewes, lounged in a swivel chair, juiced a chaw of tobacco under his tongue, and spat occasionally in the general direction of a brass spittoon.

"I need to see Drogovich's wires," he said.

"That's confidential. Company policy."

Toole sighed. "The policy seems to depend on how much of a tip you get."

"You suggesting I can be bought?"

"Clewes. How about you taking a break for a few minutes?"

"Nope, I'm on duty."

Toole felt too tired to argue. He reached for the outgoing messages stabbed onto a wicked-looking spindle and found Drogovich's near the top.

"You got a search warrant from Pericles Shaw?"

"Nope. Neither does Drogovich. I saw him reading my wires and all-points bulletins."

"Well, confound it, you put that down." Clewes's protests weren't very compelling, but the brown glob he fired at Toole's boots spoke louder.

Toole ignored him. Drogovich had sent one more wire, to a Porter McGuire at a Last Chance Gulch address. "Robbed near Miles City Filomena taken. Hire special train send entire outfit. Check Attabury and report fast."

That was all. But Toole had a name. Attabury.

"Clewes, send a message, bill the county. To the sheriff at Helena." He penciled a message in capital letters and handed it to Clewes. NP ROBBERY SUSPECT NAMED ATTABURY FROM HELENA. SEND INFORMATION. ALSO ANYONE NAMED CON CONNECTED TO ATTABURY.

"You plumb stole that," Clewes said. "I'm not responsible. I'll tell Drogovich that."

"Tell him what you want. Just send it, and fast."

Clewes swiveled grudgingly to the silent key. Not much wire traffic kept it ticking at four in the morning.

"When you get a reply send someone at once," Toole said. "I'll be at home."

Toole didn't wait. He clutched the stack of statements taken from mulcted passengers and plunged into a gray premonition of day, walking with leaden legs through a lonely sporting district to Main, and then north to his white cottage, worries about Mimi crowding his fogged brain.

He found her sitting in his surgery, bundled in a robe, his double-barreled shotgun across her lap. It darted upward and then lowered again as he entered.

"Oh, Santo."

"You all right?"

"No. I'll never be all right."

She didn't rise; she didn't come to hug him. Instead, she pulled the lapel of her robe tighter about her neck.

"Mimi—" he began.

She stared back at him with a wild eye. "Don't say anything. I don't like men. Why can't you just be a doctor?"

He wanted to tell her the robbers came for a doctor, not a sheriff, but he said nothing. Instead, he plucked the evil blue-barreled weapon from her grasp and set it aside. Then he gently lifted her to her feet and drew her to him. She stood rigidly.

"I'm so glad you're safe, Mimi. My God, how I worried."

She didn't yield. And then she did. She slumped into him, clutching fiercely, and he felt the wetness of tears. Slowly her anger melted in the safe circle of his arms, and her own clutched him closer and closer, as if she could not bear to let go.

He led her by the hand back to their bedroom. Sliced rawhide cord lay on the plank floor, a relic of the night's indignities. The bedclothes lay scattered. The room that had been their sanctuary had a feel about it of a railroad station. He pulled her into the bed and started to undo her robe, but she wouldn't surrender it. He drew her to him until her head nestled into his shoulder and her silky jet hair fell over his chest. It was enough. She'd talk when she could. His clawing questions could wait.

"I've lost my privacy. Now they'll all whisper about me. Now they'll—be familiar."

He couldn't think of a way to comfort her. A woman's modesty could be as precious to her as pearls.

"Catch them! Throw them in jail forever!" she muttered. "Cut their eyes out. That's what my mother would do. Torture them slowly, eyes first."

Whenever Mimi was terribly angry, she found solace in her Assiniboin mother's ways.

"How were you freed?" he ventured, after they had clung to each other in the dusky dawn a long time.

"I heard someone. They pounded. They came around and looked in the horse barn. They rapped on windows. I couldn't do anything. I lay here with my hands tied behind my back, my feet tied. I—didn't want them to see me anyway, whoever they were."

"The conductor and a passenger. One who'd lost a fortune to them."

She buried herself into the hollow of his shoulder again. "I didn't want them to see me. I'm yours, Santo. Everything is yours. My body—it's yours. My heart and soul are yours. I didn't want them to come in . . . But I hurt so much. My hands—they'd gone numb. The cord was so tight. I couldn't feel anything. I thought my hands would die. Oh, Santo, I didn't want—anyone—I'm yours alone."

"You'll always be. And I for you."

He felt the wetness again. "But I had to get free!" she whispered. "I swung my feet down. I got to the floor and thumped. I banged with my heels. They heard it. I was so—ashamed."

"Graves—the conductor—freed you?"

"Yes. He threw a blanket over me first. And apologized. But I was so glad to be free. My hands stung and prickled. Life came back to them. Oh, Santo. After that I was so afraid for you. Until they sent word." She gripped him a moment. "I almost shot the brakeman," she added.

"Messengers bearing good tidings shouldn't be shot," he said. "It discourages messengering."

She slid swiftly into sleep, her olive hands clutching him as she dozed off. He couldn't sleep, though he could barely keep himself awake. His mind gnawed at the trouble, but he knew he was too exhausted to plan intelligently. He could appoint a posse. He'd done that once or twice and found that the town's businessmen didn't make much of a force and resented being called away from their work. He could head out alone. He could deputize Drogovich's force—whatever and whoever they might be—and lead them. The latter thought chilled him. A man like Drogovich would have an army like Drogovich, and Toole would find himself along for the sole purpose of tacking a legal veneer to a lynching.

Sunlight foiled his hopes of sleep, and he finally crawled out of bed feeling robbed of rest and testy. His bride, lost in sleep at last, languidly searched the empty place where he'd lain, and sighed. He drew lukewarm water from the stove reservoir and lathered the brown stubble of beard with his shaving brush. He honed his razor on the wide Nero strop and began scraping, not enjoying the morning ritual.

That's when the booming of his front door confronted him. He slid his suspenders over his cotton underdrawers and opened it to Drogovich.

"Toole. Get saddled. We'll go look," Drogovich announced.

The man looked as if three hours of sleep was all he'd ever need. Behind him a livery barn saddler stood with one leg cocked, tied to the hitching post.

Toole yawned. "Mr. Drogovich. I have patients. I have morning rounds. I got no rest. I'm tired."

"You're a do-nothing, Toole. Drogovich admires men who act. We're going for a little ride. My special comes in around noon. We've six hours to pick up a trail. I'll saddle your horse while you put yourself together."

"Go pick up a trail yourself," Toole said. "You seem to know how to do everything."

"I know how to use men. And I'm using you."

Toole yawned. "If I go out, I'll go alone. And if your private army arrives while I'm gone, hold them. I'll not have a band of armed riders loose in my county."

"I'm coming with you. I'll tell you about Attabury. Oh, Drogovich read your wire, Toole. And I got it from Clewes that you read mine. First sensible thing you did all night."

"Who's Attabury?"

"I'll tell you later."

"Is he polite?"

"I'll tell you when we're out. We're going to pick up that trail before my men arrive. It must be a foot deep in mud."

"It might not exist at all, Drogovich."

"You have any better plan, Sheriff?"

In fact he didn't. And in fact he might get some pieces of the puzzle out of Drogovich while they rode.

"All right. Saddle my gray. Be careful. He's a feisty Irish thoroughbred. I'll be with you directly, Drogovich."

The man grinned. Embers burned in his eyes. "You micks," he said.

Ingmar Drogovich enjoyed his little secret. He knew something Toole didn't know. He knew who'd robbed the train, or at least who the principals were. That morning, he'd crossed the road separating Macqueen House from the station, caught Clewes just when he was surrendering his bailiwick to the day man, and pulled yellow flimsies off the spindle. He read Toole's wire with interest: Who was Attabury, a suspect? And did the Helena sheriff connect him to a Con someone?

That told him everything: Constantine Luce, the former superintendent of the Fate. So it had been Attabury and Luce. It surprised him, but not a whole lot. He'd studied men over his lifetime and he'd learned that most of them were capable of anything. They'd struck back. Robbing passengers had been camouflage.

Drogovich had Clewes send one last wire before departing, a simple word to Yablonski, sheriff of Lewis and Clark County and the law around Last Chance Gulch. That's all it took. Toole would learn nothing about Con Luce; little about Attabury. That wire didn't go on the spindle nor did it enter the records.

They rode over heavy ground, gumbo sucking each hoof and tiring their mounts. Drogovich let Toole lead. They followed a dirt trail along the track, with scarcely a dimple in it to demark the passage of animals before the storm. Eventually Toole turned toward the south bluffs and the footing got better. Dun rock underlay their trail as they climbed toward the rough plains above the wide trench of the Yellowstone.

"This where they took you?" he asked.

"Yes. Blindfolded. I didn't know it until they took me to a place I knew."

"You must have known you were climbing."

"I knew it was the south bluffs, yes. We didn't go north

because of the Yellowstone. If we'd gone west, I'd have heard us cross the military bridge or ford the Tongue River.''

''You shouldn't have gone at all.''

''You told me that. And I told you I am bound by oath to help any man in distress—including a robber.''

''You're sentimental, Toole. Irish are like that.''

''Any man worth something is like that. I go where I'm needed, and do what my soul requires.''

Drogovich measured the man. ''Your ideals have a practical side. You got to see them; hear them; treat one. You have a good idea what they're like.''

''Yes. I got some clues. But I'd have gone anyway; done what I could to repair flesh and ease pain, even for nothing.''

''No wonder you're poor and live in a cottage and wrestle with two miserable jobs. Most people leave boyhood behind, eh?''

''And superstition too, Drogovich. We Irish are full of saints and sin, and we're all poor as a country parson. Half the time we're on the side of the outlaws.''

Ingmar Drogovich didn't like what he was hearing. Idealists were the enemy of progress. Their scruples got in the way of practical living. You couldn't buy or bribe them the way you could buy more flexible men, and you couldn't blackmail them either, unless you could trump something up. He sighed unhappily. This fool mick would interfere. He had plans. The one thing he didn't want was for Attabury and his gang to be brought to trial. It'd bring certain things to light, such as how the Fate was wrested from Attabury. In Helena it wouldn't matter much; a word to old Judge Smythe would bury the matter. But things might be different here.

''Drogovich admires a man of principle,'' he said. ''It's so rare.''

''A man sees himself in the mirror when he scrapes his face in the morning,'' Toole said. ''He knows what's behind the stubble. I've made my choices. Accidentally, you might say. My father popped me in medical school. I had no inclination for it, at least not until Lister got ahold of me and taught me antiseptics and surgery. Then he shipped me to

America. I'm the youngest son, you see. We don't inherit. The medical education came in lieu of remittances. Neither he—saints preserve him—nor I, imagined I'd take it seriously."

They rode over corrugated prairie in a direction known only to the sheriff, leaving a clear trail of hoofprints in the soft clay. The morning had turned golden, with a cool breeze and a June sun coaxing the boisterous grasses. Ingmar Drogovich noticed. He prided himself on noticing everything, and was not insensitive to the glory of this cool day.

"Now who's Attabury?" Toole asked.

"A Helena geologist and engineer."

"And why'd you seek to know his whereabouts?"

"He's no friend of Drogovich."

"Ah, no friend. A business acquaintance." Toole was waiting for more, but Drogovich didn't feel like elaborating. "He robbed you. Why would he do that, Drogovich?"

"I don't know that he did. That gang cleaned out all the passengers. Banged one on his thick skull. It could have been ordinary train robbers."

"It could've been Jesse James, returned to earth."

Drogovich wasn't used to being mocked, especially by a mick. He turned and stared at Toole, seeing a man too slender to be enforcing law and too bright to be in a frontier village.

They rode quietly, seeing nothing, cutting no tracks. Toole didn't seem to expect them to. At last Toole rode around the base of a steep hill and paused at some sort of settlement. A soddy had been cut into a slope and beside it some sort of lean-to.

"Here," Toole said, drawing up and dismounting. He tied his gray to a hitchrail. Drogovich followed, peering at a place that showed no sign of habitation. The sod roof had melted under rain, and soon would collapse. "Murphy's place. Sheepherder. Either got chased out or murdered a while ago, I never knew which."

"This where they brought you?"

Toole didn't answer, but ducked inside. Drogovich followed, recoiling from the dank smell of dirt. Someone had been here. Drogovich eyed vague footprints in the dust and a brown spot he took for dried blood.

"You treated one here?"

"Right there."

"Where was Filomena?"

"I heard noises out there." Toole pointed toward the lean-to.

They walked into it through a narrow opening, and Drogovich heard the scurrying of rodents. Some ancient straw lay on the floor amidst stone-hard droppings.

"I'm delighted she learned how the other half lives," Drogovich said, surveying the decay. "It's a lesson."

Toole grabbed a pole and began poking into ancient heaps of hay that had turned almost black with must and rot.

"What're you doing?" Drogovich asked.

"We're looking for about two hundred thousand in bullion, aren't we? And a bag of valuables or two?"

Drogovich poked around enthusiastically, kicking and poking, stomping the earth to detect the resonance of a cache. He didn't mind the grime settling into his fine-wrought black broadcloth suit. "You don't suppose they left it here," he said.

"A good sheriff doesn't suppose. He collects facts."

Drogovich grudgingly conceded the point. Maybe Toole would be worth something—if he could keep Toole under leash.

They found nothing in the lean-to. They ransacked Murphy's soddy as well, finding not a scrap of evidence other than the blood and some rearranged dust. Outside, the clay of the yard lay rain-dimpled and virginal, and the only evidence that the gang had been there was some water-soaked manure around the hitchrail. Toole kicked it, exposing its bright green interior.

"Where'd they go from here?" Drogovich asked.

Toole didn't reply but clambered up the slope behind the soddy, skidding on gumbo. Drogovich pursued heavily, not wanting to sully his suit any further.

Toole reached the apex of the hill and studied the country carefully. Drogovich did too, seeing nothing. The virgin land glowed in summer sun and hid all marks of passage.

"We've three hundred sixty degrees to choose from," Toole said. "But if this was Attabury's party, I suppose they'd be heading west to Helena. You might go back and meet them there."

The mock had returned to the mick. Drogovich noted it and noted that in a few hours there'd be no mick mock. Not around his outfit.

"They might have flown out," Toole said. "Jesse James would be inclined to fly."

Drogovich ignored him. "Toole. Horses leave tracks. Even in a downpour. I want a trail now, before the special arrives."

"We'll invent one," Toole said, his eyes too bright.

They rode a spiral around Murphy's dugout, finding nothing, the mick sheriff studying every sagebrush in amused silence. They spiraled out again, this time in a half-mile arc, cutting no sign. Toole kept to himself, but Drogovich noticed that the sheriff paused at a coulee tumbling westward toward the distant valley of the Tongue.

"May as well," Toole said, steering his gray into the shallow vee. "It's the best bet—which isn't saying much."

Chapter 7

A sorrier band of successful brigands never rode the back-trails of the West. They catnapped, let their horses graze, and then rode again at mid-morning. Elwood had to lift Luce into the saddle. The superintendent looked gray but clasped the saddle horn gamely. Chico helped Filomena up. She rode astride, her narrow skirts hiked high, baring a shapely calf. She enjoyed his stare and the gaze of the rest. She looked uncommonly beautiful in the glowing morning, though the rest looked uncommonly haggard.

They rode silently, leaving their mark behind them in the soft clay of the treeless plains. They rode westward over rough prairie, paralleling the Yellowstone but miles north of the river and its traffic. Not a tree was visible from horizon to horizon.

They'd intended either to wear bandannas over their faces or blindfold Filomena as long as they had her; but it seemed foolish now. She might not know their names, but she knew who they were. They were her prisoners far more than she was theirs.

They had, Elwood knew, no place to go. Certainly they couldn't go back to Helena and pick up life where they'd dropped it. That'd been the plan once, an eternity ago. Slip away; slip back in, each with an alibi. Sequester the loot for six months, until the memory of the distant robbery dimmed.

He sighed, thinking of the innocence in all that. He'd taken to banditry like a schoolboy, though the others had been less sanguine about it. He rode clouded in gloom until at last he realized it wasn't helpful. They might yet triumph. He had no religion to speak of, but he had a stern discipline, the fruit of his New England puritan roots. He resolved to put his strengths to use or all would be lost. Resolutely he reviewed his problems: escape was the first and most important enterprise. The second was to find some way to deal with Filomena. Third, the failing body of Constantine Luce. And finally, demoralization among them all, which could turn this escape into chaos and pain.

He couldn't do anything about Con Luce—unless they came upon a place to hide Luce until he healed. But all his other problems were tractable. He might shake his pursuers. He might handle Filomena. Surely there'd be ways to return to Helena and live there quietly. And surely he could buck up the flagging spirits of these good men who'd done something that now anguished them.

He reined up his horse, waited for Filomena, and then rode beside her trying to keep his eyes and mind off those long, shapely legs that vanished into a froth of petticoat just above the knee.

"I have good legs," she said. "And the rest of me matches them."

Elwood Attabury III had never heard talk like that from mortal woman, at least the respectable sort. He blushed. She was smiling, some golden Slavic beauty softening the strong planes of her face.

"I'm Elwood Attabury, amateur bandit," he said. "And former owner of the Fate. I'm a mining engineer from Massachusetts. Your father and I are all too well acquainted."

"I'm too well acquainted with him also."

"These gentlemen all encountered—difficulties. Because of your father."

"They aren't alone," she said. "He makes difficulties. It's his calling. It's my calling also, like a nun's vow. I do it from boredom."

"We're your prisoners," he said.

That puzzled her a moment. She laughed cheerfully, green eyes gazing toward him and suddenly away.

"You hold us in your thrall. We wear no masks, you see. Your prisoner over there is Karl Astleheim, a powder man. The best powder man in this republic, I'll wager. He says the beginning of wisdom is that an explosive force expands equally in all directions. He says it's an analogy for life. He thinks your father's an explosive force."

He had her attention now, and she listened curiously. This occupied her better than banter.

"The wounded man is Constantine Luce, superintendent of the Fate—until your father took it away. He may not be your prisoner long."

She eyed Con Luce, who slumped heavily over his saddle. Her bright assessment turned solemn.

"Now your prisoner back there, the one with the pack-horses carrying our plunder, is Chico. He's Welsh, and how he got his name is a mystery. A born miner. A mucker who's shoveled countless tons of ore into cars. He loved the mine mules and cared for them. He loves horseflesh and knows exactly what an animal will endure. Your father's plug-uglies hurt him.

"Beside him rides Enrico Ferrero. He's a driller. You can tell it from his shoulders. A singlejack man. He's particularly your prisoner because he has a wife and five children in Helena. And he, like these others, remains loyal to me at great cost. Your father refused to employ him—and saw to it that no other mine in the district employed him. His children starve. Three have consumption. If you want to make difficulties, why, he's a prime victim."

Her gaze met his and held it. He didn't flinch, though he might have just one day earlier. Something steely was being forged inside of Elwood Attabury III.

"And the remaining gentleman, the slender and sun-burned one there, is my bookkeeper, Angus Dillingham. Angus the Righteous, I call him. Your father wished him to perjure himself before the courts and offered him a nosegay for it. Angus the Righteous turned into Angus the Wrathful and told your father things I shan't repeat. He'd turn red if he heard his own words, spoken, of course, in a moment of

Scots temper. He can no longer find employment in the whole district. He, too, is the prisoner of your mischief.''

"What words? I'm one to improve my vocabulary if I can. We operate at a disadvantage, you know. I mean, women do. I know my father's collection but my experience of them is limited. He won't let me go into the pit. I don't enunciate them properly, but perhaps you can train me. I'll whisper one and you tell me what it means.''

"You have me there, Miss Drogovich.''

"And you?'' she asked, surveying him closely, as if to see him for the first time.

"Me? I'm an amateur bandit,'' he said. "It's not the vocation I had in mind back in Boston. But the West does something to a person. Loosens the strings. You can't live here without changing.''

"I think I prefer the East. I was about to find out—before this detour.''

"Why the East?''

"The men. I'm an old maid. I've decided not to marry, but I wouldn't mind keeping a proper man. Provided he was sufficiently insulting.''

"Ah . . . Why Eastern men?''

"Western men are pansies.''

That wasn't the answer he expected. But then, nothing about her was what he'd expected even though her reputation preceded her. He studied her furtively as they rode, admiring her porcelain complexion, glittering—and dangerous—green eyes, and kinked brass hair. Her bare calves drew his gaze and tickled audacious thoughts in him.

The nakedness of the land brought him intimacy. Whenever they topped a swell, the infinities of the plains subdued them. It was as if the hazy horizons didn't stretch to known places, geographical points, but to altered lives. Luce rode along unaware, his hands death-clawing the saddle horn, but the rest rode in somber silence through an oceanic void full of sage and bunchgrass. Filomena seemed even more eager for conversation than Elwood, discomfited by sheer space and finding her captor a welcome shipmate. He took advantage of it.

"What is your wish?" he asked.

"My wish? To shoot you dead."

"What would you like us to do with you?"

"Take me to the nearest settlement with a wire and a sheriff. I'll tattle on you, right down to the buttons on your britches, and then go east."

"You make it hard for us to release you."

"I make things hard for everyone. As I told you, that's my vocation. I'm bored and have little better to do. Being a pest is entertainment for me. Suffering is entertainment. They call me a terror in Last Chance Gulch. The pansies, I mean."

"Well then, you can work your torments on me. Poor Con, there, is beyond caring. I am good at enduring. I am especially good at enduring women. It comes from long familiarity."

"Are you married?"

"No, thank heaven," he said. "I take my meals in cafés and have a housekeeper."

They topped a subtle shoulder and began the long descent into the drainage of Porcupine Creek which lay like a green thread upon the horizon. He lapsed into silence, wondering what to do with her; wondering if there was anything to do. He itched simply to unload her right there; let her make her way back or forward, survive or not survive. But he couldn't do that: it'd be murder.

An hour later Con Luce slid off his horse.

Santiago was swiftly coming to a decision. He would share nothing with the powerful man beside him. Whatever he learned would remain locked in his own mind. His initial instinct had been to work in harness with the gold king, whose own resources might lead Santiago directly to the train robbers. It seemed at first a good idea, a way to multiply his powers.

But now, after a fruitless morning alongside a baronial figure who seemed to toy with him and conceal more than he revealed, Toole changed his mind. He'd asked again who Attabury was, but Drogovich would tell him only that Attabury was a Helena mining man. He'd asked Drogovich how he'd acquired his mine, and Drogovich had replied that he'd bought it. From whom? From its owners. He'd asked Drogovich what his daughter's habits were and how she might endure captivity or worse. And that had netted him a laugh. Some velvet curtain had descended, leaving Toole in the dark. Whatever Drogovich's life and affairs had been in distant Helena, they were beyond Santiago's reach.

His mind made up, Santiago said nothing when his eye caught a bit of green manure caught in sagebrush as they descended the long coulee sliding toward the Tongue River. He said nothing to Drogovich. The great man didn't seem to notice it, perhaps because he was looking for fresh tracks and finding not a dimple in the wet clay.

But if the train robbers had come this way, they were heading westward. If they were antagonists of Drogovich, they'd probably end up in Helena, following the south bank of the Yellowstone as far as they could. He made a note to have sheriffs in counties to the west talk to the several ferrymen. In this flood month, when the Yellowstone carried mountain winter away, a fording by horses laden with gold would be most unlikely. Chances were, if the robbers were heading west they wouldn't ford until Clark City—they were calling it Livingston now—when they had to because the river turned south. He'd wire, and he'd keep the copy off the telegrapher's spindle.

When they reached the narrow valley of the Tongue, Drogovich extracted a gold pocket watch from his waistcoat and examined it.

"How far are we from Miles?" he asked.

"About five miles."

"We'd better get back. These nags are tired. And we'll just make the special if my information's right."

"The horses are tired all right, Drogovich. You seem to know something of horseflesh."

"I do. Have my own racing stable. Kentucky stock. I run

them in match races against Daly over in Butte City. So far, copper's bought better horseflesh than gold, but I'm working on it.''

"Your daughter rides?"

"Expertly."

"Could she escape on horse?"

Drogovich laughed.

Faintly irked, Toole rode toward Miles over the dimpled clay of the river trace. It showed little sign of a night passage. He felt his thoroughbred labor, and knew that Drogovich's livery barn horse was worse off. Drogovich probably weighed fifteen stone.

"Drogovich. The rain's scoured this country. Have you a clue where the robbers are heading?"

"Drogovich has good men coming."

The man had ducked again. Toole rode silently north, too weary to enjoy a fresh June morning. He dozed in the saddle until awakened by a shrill whistle. Ahead lay the trestle over the Tongue, and approaching it was a straight-stacked engine flying two white flags. It pulled a coach and a boxcar and crummy. Even as it thundered out upon the wooden scaffolding, its brakes caught the drive wheels and its piston steam scythed the cross-ties.

"There you are," Toole muttered. "Listen, Drogovich. There'll be firm rules. I don't like the idea of an armed gang of men running around my county. I have no intention of deputizing them. If they fail to conduct themselves as private citizens should, they'll be in big trouble."

Drogovich paid him no heed. The man heeled the livery stable chestnut into a weary lope, heading for the station a half mile ahead. Toole didn't hurry his gray, choosing instead to weigh the man. He was sure Drogovich heard him—and sure Drogovich ignored him. It didn't augur well.

Off to the east the special screeched to a halt, hissing and belching like a colicky dinosaur. Ahead, Drogovich's horse balked at the rails, but Drogovich expertly angled the animal over one rail and finally over the other, not far behind the halted train. Then Drogovich disappeared from sight, hidden by the green caboose.

Toole halted near the trestle and studied the place. He was rewarded at once by the sight of fresh prints leading to the river's edge, prints dappling soft clay that had been protected from the battering rain by the trestle. Even from where he stood he could see them again on the west bank, heading north. It hadn't been a futile morning after all. But until he took the measure of the hard men getting off that maroon coach, he had no intention of sharing his discovery. He toyed with the thought of slipping off alone while he had the chance. But he rejected it. He had to know at once what sort of armed men Drogovich had imported into Custer County.

He rode wearily toward the station, expecting to see a posse forming up on the platform, armed men in all-weather gear awaiting swift instructions. Instead, he found a few city slickers lounging about. And not a posse in sight. Drogovich had vanished, but his horse stood at a hitching post. Toole counted seven men. They wore lumpy double-breasted suits, some of plain broadcloth shiny at the elbows, others with chalky stripes. One was bareheaded; the rest wore bowlers. He saw no weapons, but a closer look at the odd bulges in the suit coats of these burly gents persuaded him that he'd find small revolvers in shoulder holsters among them, knouts, saps, brass knuckles, various stilettos and other species of urban mayhem on their persons.

Of course, he thought. Drogovich would scarcely have plainsmen doing his bidding in Helena. The whole lot of them looked as odd in a prairie cow town as a cowboy might look at Delmonico's in New York. They looked pale, as if they'd emerged out of the night and lived in sunless places. They radiated an odd menace, and he didn't doubt that they comprised a formidable army at Drogovich's beck and call. They eyed him casually, seeing no menace in a slim, haggard man on a thin horse.

A whinny erupted from the boxcar, and Santiago knew that his own horse on the cinder station platform had excited some horses in the car. He puzzled the reason they still remained in the boxcar, and could find no reason for it unless these plug-uglies didn't know enough about horses even to exercise the animals. He wondered if any could ride, and found himself wishing they couldn't.

Toole tied his horse and walked past them, feeling their assessments as he did. He wasn't wearing his star. He pierced into the waiting room and headed for the stationmaster's offices, knowing he'd find Drogovich there, scanning incoming wires—including those addressed to Toole—and paying no attention to the day telegrapher.

Drogovich stood there, a sheaf of flimsies in hand, enjoying his survey of privy information. Beside him stood another of his cronies, this one sallow to the point of jaundice, in a black suit that hung so loosely that the man had obviously lost weight. The day wireman, Cecil Varney, spotted Toole and shrugged. Toole understood the gesture.

"Toole. Meet Arnold Carp," Drogovich said. "He's in charge."

Carp extended a clammy hand, which Santiago grasped and dropped.

"Reading the mail again, Drogovich."

"Here's yours, Toole," he said, thrusting several at Santiago.

One, from the N.P.'s regional offices in Bismarck, informed Sheriff Toole that the railroad was dispatching private investigators who would arrive on the noon westbound. They would cooperate with him. Three others, from assorted lawmen, requested physical descriptions of the robbers and the hostage woman, if known. The remaining wire, from Lewis and Clark County sheriff Yablonski, said he'd look into the name Attabury and reply. And as for someone named Con, there must be a hundred in Helena.

"Friend of yours, Yablonski?" Toole asked.

"No. Drogovich owns him."

"You own a sheriff and an army."

"You needn't worry about them, Toole. They're not staying."

"Not staying?"

"Not in your county, Toole. They're going back a hundred miles and wait. A little trap."

"Back west? Up the river?"

"Out of your county, Toole. Soon as the railroad switches the engine and caboose."

"Drogovich," Toole said. "Come with me to my offices. I've something to discuss."

"Drogovich never has time."

"I think you'd better come." He turned to Carp. "You too."

The pair exchanged glances and reluctantly followed Toole up Sixth Street. He hiked briskly through the sporting district to Main and then east to the stone edifice that served as Toole's office. Toole let them in and reached for a loaded shotgun on the rack behind his battered desk.

"All right, tell me what you know," he said. "Or sit in there"--he nodded at the cellroom door at the rear—"until you do. I don't know that the robbers are heading west, but you do. I don't know what connection they have with you, but you do. Tell me—or rot in there."

Carp eyed him with faint amusement, but Drogovich's eyes burned like coals in hell.

Chapter 8

Incredulity suffused the face of Ingmar Drogovich. "Toole," he said, "I happen to be the victim."

"Maybe," Toole agreed. "If you won't talk, get in there." He waved the muzzle of the twelve-gauge toward the empty jailroom.

Drogovich did nothing. Carp smiled slightly, his hand crawling up toward the bosom of his suit coat.

"Don't," Toole said.

"You wouldn't," said Carp, his hand continuing its progress.

Toole lifted the shotgun and fired. The ear-splitting blast rocked the small room. Plaster from the mauled ceiling careened over them. In the percussive shock, Toole lifted his revolver from its nest while Carp stood, paralyzed and white-faced. Toole's ears rang, and he knew the others were suffering from the indoor concussion.

"I'll be damned," muttered Carp.

"Inside," he said.

"For what crime?" Drogovich asked, heavily.

"You're accessories, after the fact. Withholding information from a duly constituted officer of the law investigating a crime."

The gold magnate absorbed that slowly. "Toole. Remember. I'm Drogovich. Remember that. You're going to remember it."

"In," Toole said.

They didn't move.

"Peel your suit coats off—slowly."

Both did, letting them drop. Carp's clanked on the planks.

A small revolver nestled in a rig under Carp's left shoulder. "Lean against that wall with your arms out, back to me."

They leaned. Toole plucked Carp's revolver from the man, wary of sudden swift motion. He patted them swiftly, finding nothing more. Menace radiated from Drogovich even with his back turned.

"Now. In," Toole said. "Or get hurt."

They obeyed. He locked them in separate cells.

"I want a lawyer, Toole. Now. And when Drogovich is out, you'll know it."

"Glad to be warned," Toole said. "You can leave anytime you tell me everything you know. Like, who's Attabury? Who's a man named Con? Where do they live? Why did they rob you and take your daughter? What's your business association with them? How do you know they're heading west? Why did your sheriff over there duck my requests for information? And what do you plan to do with these crooks? Think about it. You know things that the sheriff of Custer County doesn't know. You're hiding them, and that makes you accessories. I'm going to the judge—Pericles Shaw—for warrants."

"Toole. I'm posting a thousand-dollar award for the capture of those train robbers—whoever they might be."

"Drogovich. Bribing an officer of the law is a criminal offense. I'll add that to the charge."

"You're dealing with Ingmar Drogovich."

"I never heard of you until last night."

"You'll never forget me."

He locked the cell-room door. He reloaded the shotgun and placed it in its rack. He eyed the ruined ceiling. The county fathers would take it out of his sixty a month. He locked the front door and stepped into a clean bright day, letting the sun and azure sky scour away his anger.

He hastened over to the old sandstone courthouse and found Pericles Shaw in his cubbyhole of an office, perusing

Caesar's *Commentaries*, tiny half glasses perched on his bulbous nose.

"I heard a racket from your lair," Shaw said.

"I've jailed the victim of a train robbery."

"There's a novelty. Is it a misdemeanor or a felony?"

"Both. I want warrants. First, a John Doe for parties unknown who robbed the eastbound last night. They murdered the expressman, injured a passenger, abducted a passenger, robbed passengers of valuables, and stole bullion from the express car. Oh, yes. And abducted me. Tied up Mimi."

"And you've jailed the victims. Santiago, you get more entertaining every day."

"I want two more warrants, for an Ingmar Drogovich and an Arnold Carp. Obstructing justice. Impeding a law officer in his investigation. Accessories after the fact."

"You forgot spitting on public streets."

"They forgot to spit."

"And you forgot discharging a firearm within city limits."

"That's my crime, Pericles."

"With intent to kill?"

"I killed the plaster of the ceiling."

"Ah. A misdemeanor. The county supervisors will have their way with you. Drogovich, you say? The gold man?"

"The same."

"How'd he take his incarceration?"

"Tried to bribe me, but I can't prove it. And told me I'd never forget him. We've another little problem. He brought his private army over. Some plug-uglies hanging around the depot. A mean bunch if ever I saw one. He wanted me to deputize them, but now he tells me he's pulling them out of the county. Pericles, he's got enough firepower over there so we might need help from the army."

"If they're leaving, I see no problem."

"As long as Drogovich is enjoying my hospitality—and Carp—they're a problem."

"You have a point, Santiago. Well, manufacture the papers and I'll put my John Henry on them." He waved toward a stack of warrant forms and the ink pot. He peered over his half spectacles. "You'll have to arraign them, you know. Better do it fast, before the uglies catch on."

"I'm getting help. Some railroad dicks on the westbound from Bismarck."

Toole found a steel nib and began scratching out warrants; six John Does and two others for Drogovich and Carp. Old Pericles looked them over and endorsed them. A train whistle wailed off to the south. The N.P. special was turned around and ready, Toole supposed. And summoning its passengers. He waved the paper in the sultry air to dry the ink, and then folded the warrants into his breast pocket. He'd arraign Drogovich. Then see some patients he'd neglected. Then deal with the plug-uglies.

"I enjoy your humor, Toole. I never would have thought to throw the victims into the pokey. It opens up new vistas of justice."

Toole ignored him and plunged into the sunlight again. Moments later he found the door of the sheriff office unlocked—and company within. Five gents in bowlers and ill-fitting suits studying him. And Drogovich and Carp. The cell-room door was ajar.

"Well, Dr. Toole," Drogovich said.

Santiago stared at them all. One or another was a genius with locks. "Breaking and entering. That's a crime. Jailbreak's a bigger crime."

"Why, Toole, no one's run off."

"Jailbreak. Felony," Toole said.

"I'm Drogovich."

"I've warrants for you and Carp. We'll go arraign you."

Drogovich laughed. That was a clue for the chorus to laugh. They wheezed and chortled, and one laughed silently, a chain of hiccoughs erupting from his meaty frame.

"Warrants, Toole? Warrants?"

"Unless you want to tell me what you know."

"A warrant for Drogovich." The ember coals in the man's eyes flared up again. "A Custer County warrant for Ingmar Drogovich. Surely it's a case of mistaken identity."

"All right. Let's go to court. The judge is Pericles Shaw. It's up to him to quash the warrants, not me."

"Pericles Shaw. Pericles Shaw. The name is unknown to Drogovich. Tear them up, Toole. This never happened. It's better that way. For Drogovich. For you. For Pericles Shaw."

"A sheriff can't tear up a warrant."

"Let me see it."

Toole knew what was about to happen to the warrants. And what would happen if he resisted. As if to punctuate Drogovich's demand, one of the uglies slid brass knuckles over his meaty hand, a finger through each of the four holes. The man's hand had turned into a lethal weapon. Toole had scarcely seen brass knuckles before, and stared, mesmerized, at the simple instrument that could pulverize his flesh while protecting the user. Toole's gaze lifted from the hand as it clenched and unclenched, up to a blank face, inscrutable except for pinpoints of white light flaring in the man's watery eyes.

Toole pulled the warrants from his breast pocket, his Irish up. But fear subdued even his sharp anger. He handed the sheaf to Drogovich, ashamed of his deepening terror.

"Ah, thank you, Toole. You have pleased Drogovich, and he doesn't forget. He never forgets anything. He's like the Bourbons of France who never forget."

"And never learn," Toole snapped.

A fine wheezing chortle rustled through Drogovich like a passing zephyr as he tucked the warrants, including the John Doe, into his suit coat. There, Toole thought, they were protected better than in a bank vault.

The engine whistled again. "Our quarry escapes us, Toole. At least for the moment. We must leave."

"It's still jailbreak. A felony charge against every one of you."

"Drogovich is doing you a service, Toole. There's nothing more you need do. Go practice your medicine. The Fate bullion will be restored to Drogovich. The valuables of the passengers will be returned to you for distribution."

"And?"

"Pop your pills, Toole."

"Drogovich, if you think I'm going to sit here and let this happen after you've gone—"

"Oh, you will, you will. Drogovich has invited Mrs. Toole to join him. She's quite excited. The prospect of seeing the train robbers come to justice—after what they did to you— brings a brightness to her eyes."

Cold dread filtered through Toole. "Drogovich, if it's the last thing I do on this earth—"

"She finds the adventure quite pleasant, Toole. She's in the coach with my other colleagues. She wants you to understand she's safe and sound. She wants to have her lark. She doesn't need you."

Mimi on the train, abducted by the other two uglies. Mimi, his own Mimi. "Drogovich. I'll kill you."

"Drogovich never forgets, Toole. You'll tend to your patients now."

"No, Drogovich."

"No? No? You mean you want to ruin Mrs. Toole's holiday?"

Toole choked on his own rage. A sob built in him, and he swallowed it down. He knew he was berserk inside. But deep within him caution cried out—not for himself, but for Mimi. He blinked back tears and leaned into his desk.

"Medicine is a fine vocation, Toole. You understand."

Toole nodded. He understood.

"You tend to your medicine, Toole. Mrs. Toole is beautiful, don't you think? She has such a lovely face."

The engine of the special whistled again. The owner of the Fate smiled, bowed slightly, and departed into a brilliant sun. Carp followed. The other gentlemen touched fingers to their derbies in respect and walked through the door.

Murder. Toole slumped in his sheriff lair, surrounded by instruments of death. The doctor part of him had vanished. The sheriff part of him had vanished also, along with the civilized man and Christian. What remained, now subduing his brain, rose from out of the Celtic mists, from the dark fens and smoldering peat bogs of his primordial soul. Santiago Toole plotted murder. He saw it all in his mind's eye, the waiting and stalking, the slab-cheeked graying man in the buckhorn sights of his rifle somewhere around Helena, the squeeze of the trigger, the report and jolt into his shoulder, the slow reel of a collapsing mortal, the writhing on the muddy street, the systematic loading of another cartridge, the systematic aiming, squeezing, firing, and the final spasm of that body in the manure of the street. Murder.

He scarcely heard the chuffing departure of the special a few blocks south, the mounting pulse of its pistons as it built speed, and the fading melancholic rattle as it left Miles City behind. He didn't hear these things, but in his mind's eye he saw Mimi in that coach, stiff and frightened, rigid in her seat, surrounded by eight gentlemen in cheap suits and derbies, and a ninth man whose will would not be brooked.

That's how Pericles Shaw found him.

"Toole."

Slowly Santiago emerged from murder into the present, seeing the judge before him.

"Where were you?"

Toole didn't want to tell him.

"I know where you were. You were off upon the misted shore."

Toole sighed. Pericles Shaw stood over him, waiting for him to return to earth.

"What happened?" Shaw asked. "I was privy to a dark sight from the window of my chambers. The man I took for Drogovich, surrounded by his minions, striding toward a rendezvous at the station."

"Jailbreak," Toole muttered, lowering his feet from the edge of his battered oaken desk.

"And you sit here?"

"I was contemplating murder."

"Toole, Toole. First you arrest victims. Then you dwell upon murder and ignore the jailbreak. Those whom the gods destroy, they first make mad."

"They have Mimi."

Pericles rubbed the white stubble on his jowls. He shaved every third day, claiming too much scraping cancered the flesh. He peered through the barred windows into the blinding sun on Main Street. "At the risk of prejudicing a future trial, tell me—from the beginning," he said. "I can always disqualify myself. Since you're plainly mad, and I'm only partly so, I shall weigh your words."

Santiago felt so tired, he wondered if he could recount the events that began with his abduction the previous evening, but he began in a flat monotone.

"Toole—what sort of fellow is Drogovich?"

"An odd one. He often refers to himself in the third person."

"Any clue why?"

Toole shook his head.

"I think there's two Drogoviches. And the private one's different from the public one. Like Janus, the Roman god with two heads back to back. The god of beginnings, the custodian of the universe. The beginning month's named for him. Think on it, Santiago. Maybe it'll lead somewhere."

Toole nodded. Pericles could be an old fool. Impatiently he droned on, only to have Pericles trip him.

"Polite robbers you say. And educated. Knew the proper use of *may* and *can*. Flour sacks don't conceal all that much, do they? Perhaps we have a business associate of Drogovich's attempting a revenge. Did you get a list of Drogovich's holdings?"

"I tried. The sheriff over there wasn't exactly cooperative."

"What'd you ask and what'd he reply?"

"I asked if he knew an Attabury. I got that name from reading Drogovich's wire. I asked if he knew a Con, maybe associated with an Attabury. That was the name of the injured man—probably the murderer of the expressman. They spilled it when I dressed the wound."

"There it is!"

Santiago peered at the shabby old justice, who looked more and more like a bullfrog each year.

"He sneaked a peek at your wire on the telegrapher's spindle—just as you took a gander at his. He asked his minions in Helena about Attabury's whereabouts, eh? And then he sees the name Con in your wire, and he knows something you don't know. I'll bet on it. This Con means something. And suddenly he gives up the idea that it might have been a random train robbery—especially after you two failed to find tracks.''

"I found tracks. Under the Tongue River trestle. I didn't tell him."

Something bright flared in Pericles's eyes. "You didn't tell him about the name Con either. But he found it out and rushed west to intercept the bandits—men he knows."

"With Mimi," said Toole wearily. "With Mimi and a genteel warning to mind my medicine. To let it alone or Mimi'd be—God only knows. He's going to do his own species of justice."

The bullfrog began hopping around the office as if it were a field of lily pads. "Toole, you ninny. You're an idiot, which is a grade below moron. Did they show you Mimi in captivity or did they just say they had her?"

"They just said . . . Drogovich said. Look, Pericles. That man doesn't bluff."

"The beginning of wisdom is to suppose nothing and to check facts, Sheriff Toole. It's something mentioned in law school."

Toole bolted up, glared at Pericles, and stalked out into the midday glare. Two minutes later he bowled through the gate in the picket fence and burst into his surgery, discovering Mrs. Gatz there.

"Where've you been? You always have morning hours on Thursday. I've a very painful—"

He ignored her, plunged into the rear of his cottage. "Mimi!" he cried. He surveyed the parlor, swept the kitchen and pantry, and burst into their bedroom. No Mimi. He raced outside to the necessary room.

"Mimi!" he bawled. He banged into his carriage barn and saw only horses. Then he walked leadenly back into their bedroom where the bedclothes lay in a turmoil. He knelt beside their bed, sliding his hand over the empty place of her rest, the place of their whispers, of life shared, or hurts nursed and healed, of laughter, of mourning the darkness of the world, of held hands and hungry kisses, of mutual speculation about God and fossils and sin and the number of stars. The place where she had often told him she loved him, forever, unto death and beyond death, into the chambers of departed souls.

Pericles was wrong. The marriage bed was empty.

Chapter 9

Two strangers in coarse, flappy suits and bowlers materialized in Mimi's kitchen. She stopped peeling potatoes and
turned, fear lancing her.

"Where's Mrs. Toole?" one said.

She was about to identify herself but paused. They took
her for help. White men did that. They saw the coppery
planes and jet hair of her mother's Assiniboin people and
missed the gray eyes and thin nose of her French father. She
studied them further, not liking them, noting odd bulges pro-
truding from suit coats that didn't fit around the collar.

"I don't know," she said, her mind racing through possibilities. "If you want to see the doctor, wait in the front,
please."

Her cottage had become all too porous these last few hours,
and it troubled her. Her reticule, with the little five-shot lady's revolver that Santiago had insisted she carry, lay in her
bedroom.

They didn't move. "We'll have a little lookee," one said.

"I'll find her—if she's here. She usually shops now."

"You day help?"

She nodded, concentrating on peeling the withered skin
of a root cellar potato. Her hands trembled. Oh, where was
Santiago? Three times in the space of a few hours their cottage had been invaded. She set down the paring knife and
turned to them. "Wait in front. I'll look for her. Whom shall
I tell her is calling?"

One whispered, "Just fetch her."

"Dr. Toole's hours are in the afternoon. Is it an emergency? He's either at the courthouse or at the sheriff's office."

The one wheezed. He had sandy brows that puckered together when amusement erupted from him. "Nah, we want her. Takin' her to a little soiree."

She had to reach her reticule. Even then she wasn't sure she could handle two—two brutes—like this. She dried her hands and walked slowly past them into the dining alcove and turned into the bedroom. Her reticule lay on the nightstand.

They followed.

She needed a precious moment of privacy to extract her weapon. "I'm sure Mrs. Toole would object to your presence here, sirs. She's had a trying night."

"Hey, Cap, wouldja beat that?" the other said, pointing. Cap wheezed out an accordion laugh like his colleague. The stubby finger aimed at the pair of oval tintypes of Santiago and herself, taken by Huffman, resting on the bed stand.

"He married him a redskin. It figgers. Us micks ain't particular."

She contained herself and eased, trembling, toward her reticule, plucking it up.

"Naw," the one said. "Lay 'er down. We're takin' you on a little holiday, guest of the boss."

She eyed them bleakly, dread suffusing her. "I don't wish to go on a holiday. Tell him I decline."

"You're comin'."

"I said I decline." She met their gaze steadily, refusing to budge.

"You wouldn't want to make a scene, little squaw."

"You are abducting me."

"Naw. The boss, he wants your company."

"I wish to pack. I need a change of clothes."

"You're comin' the way you be. And you're walkin' prim and proper."

"No. You'll have to drag me to—wherever you're going."

One darted at her, and she felt a meaty hand clamp her

arm like iron jaws. "Squaw, git this. Every step you don't walk, Sheriff Toole takes a lick. If we got to drag you, Toole's meat. You want meat for a husband?" He laughed. "He ain't gonna be much of a husband afterward."

She knew she'd walk. Santiago had been beaten almost to death once, the price they'd paid for his sheriff job, and she'd nursed him for weeks and months. Even now he often hurt where his ribs and arm had been broken and his mouth lacerated. Desolately she knew she'd do whatever a woman must do to spare her man.

"All right," she said.

"Boss'll enjoy seeing ya."

"Will I ever see my husband again?"

"Depends. You'n him gotta behave."

She wanted to tell the man that Santiago Toole never behaved just right, but she didn't. It might hurt Santiago. She walked to the bedroom door and they let her squeeze by them, brushing them as she passed. One's wink to the other didn't escape her.

She undid her bib apron and pulled it over her loose jet hair and laid it on a parlor chair, very out of place. They didn't stop her. Then she walked to the front room, the surgery, out into the June sun, and through the squeaking gate in her white picket fence. The squeak had often alerted her to the arrival of a patient. Then out upon the dirt of Pleasant Street. They walked on either side of her over to Sixth, and then down Sixth. At Main they came upon strollers and shoppers.

"You don't want ta," the one on her left said. "Not if you want him back whole—you git my meanin'?"

They walked through the tenderloin in the midday sun. The parlor houses lay slumbering. They were taking her to the train station. This had something to do with the robbery. On the siding a westbound train idled, an engine hissing steam, a boxcar, a coach, a caboose. This train would take her somewhere far from Santiago. A great helplessness engulfed her, the sort of helplessness her mother's people had felt these last years with the buffalo gone and the people

caged on a barren plot of ground off to the north without so
much as a doe or coyote to eat. They were dying—heartbreak
and starvation were effective killers—and so might she.

She was guided across the platform toward the dark and
yawning door of the coach. She clambered up the iron stair,
hearing its hollow clang. She found herself in a third-class
coach with hard wicker seats that had backs on hinges. Some
of the seat backs had been thrown to permit rail patrons to
face each other. Not another soul was in this coach.

"Have a seat," said one. She obeyed. The air of the coach
was rancid with the odor of spat tobacco and ancient sweat.
The hard wicker of the seat bit her body.

The other abandoned them, hurrying up Sixth Street again.

She peered out the dirt-streaked window upon people hurrying about their business in perfect liberty. How she envied
them the simple freedom of walking where they wished to
go, doing what they intended to do. All of that had been
taken from her. She studied the coach. It seemed to be pri-
vately occupied. Duffels lay scattered on seats and in the
baggage rails above. A greasy deck of cards lay on a seat.
One pair of opposed seats had a board laid across them to
turn them into a third-class version of a bunk. The railroad
conductors rented the boards, the time-honored means for
third-class passengers to sleep. And candy butchers rented
straw-stuffed pillows. But not to Indians. She eyed the necessary room at the far end and thought to lock herself in.
Later perhaps. But it would gain her nothing except another
invasion of her privacy.

Then she saw them coming, marching down Sixth toward
the station, eight in derbies and one hatless striding before
them. They wore black like the victorious warriors of her
mother's people. She recognized the hatless one even by daylight. He had come with the conductor to free her. He had
seen her naked. They clambered aboard, and at once two
shrill blasts from the chuffing engine ahead signaled the start.
This train lurched forward even before the others settled in
the wicker seats. She turned to stare out at freedom, wishing
no contact with any of them.

"Mrs. Toole."

She felt his presence as he sat beside her, and she turned.

"I'm Ingmar Drogovich."

She eyed him, seeing a willful face with massive planes and burning dark eyes, and wiry golden hair graying at the temples. The name meant nothing to her. She peered out the sooty window again, seeing telegraph poles in motion.

"You'll enjoy the company of Drogovich if you don't embarrass him."

She saw no more reason to reply than a grasshopper would reply to the bird in whose beak it rested.

"You don't wish to talk. A rarity in women. Then you will listen. I told Sheriff Toole that you would not be harmed as long as he did not pursue. It's a matter of business, that's all."

"And if he pursues?"

"I told him you'd be used first and then killed." He said it without the slightest hesitation, as if he was not describing her own humiliation and death sentence.

"You have taken away my freedom."

"For Drogovich it is purely business. All of life is business. Sometimes unfortunates get in his way. It can't be helped. Events leave their debris."

"Where are you taking this debris?"

"To a settlement called Bighorn a hundred miles west. There's a rustic inn we'll occupy."

"Why?"

"To transact business."

"What's there?"

"Two ferries. One across the Yellowstone and one across the Big Horn River. The settlement is there—at the confluence."

"When will I be free?"

"You'll enjoy Drogovich's hospitality for as long as he wishes. Don't count on ever being free—at least not in this life. You are a hostage to Fate."

The Assiniboin in her forbade tears, but the French in her

wept. "You don't know Santiago Toole," she said, and immediately wished she hadn't said it.

Filomena wondered what Elwood Attabury III would do. The amateur bandit slid off his mount and crouched beside the injured one, loosening the man's belt. Another of the robbers, the one called Chico, wheeled his ugly horse and rode back to the shoulder they'd recently surmounted to watch their backtrail.

She knew what she would do, what had to be done, but she doubted that daffy mining engineer had any notion of it. She contemplated spurring her mare and escaping. Now would be the ideal moment with the one called Con on the wet clay and the rest of them preoccupied. But she didn't. Curiosity gripped her.

"Con—is it bad?" Attabury asked. He slid a hand over the injured man's brow.

Luce nodded.

"You've a fever." He peeled Luce's britches back a bit. Filomena watched intently.

"Your gut's swollen up. Toole's drain isn't draining much. Con—can you go on a while? We'll stop at the first likely place. Anything. A cutbank, a soddy, somewhere we can hide you and get you out of the sun and wind."

"Go on, Elwood. Just leave me. Someone comes, I'll drink this." He lifted the hand that held the blue bottle in a death grip.

"No, Con. As long as you have a chance—and we can find a spot—we'll take you. Con—" Attabury's voice broke. "Con." He dug a canteen off of Luce's saddle and held it to the man's lips. Luce swallowed a gulp and another.

"Maybe it's time to say good-bye, Elwood," Luce whispered. "It's coming now. Weak as a pup. Just leave me. Leave a revolver with me."

"We're taking you with us!"

"Elwood, you know minerals and geology, but you don't know flesh and blood. I'm not hurting—got this stuff. But it's time to go. You're a damn fine man. You did it—I mean, beat the devil. Struck a blow against the old pirate.''

Filomena marveled that a dying man would try to bolster the spirits of the living.

Attabury stood. ''Angus. You're light. I want you to ride double on Con's horse. Hold him up.''

Dillingham looked doubtful. ''It'll wear out that horse—''

''As long as there's life in Con, we'll take him along, Angus. For him—but also for us.''

The man seemed determined. Filomena gave him credit for that. Dillingham didn't argue. He turned his reins over to Ferrero and clambered onto Luce's horse back of the cantle. Then Attabury and Astleheim lifted Luce up and settled him in the saddle again.

''Watch 'er. Don't spill a drop of this stuff,'' Luce gasped. The blue bottle of laudanum had become his salvation, his religion, his hope of heaven.

They started out again, with each of them keeping to himself in the imminence of death. They rode for an hour without a word passing their lips, through a June afternoon marked only by the passage of crows. Once in a while, from shoulders, they could glimpse the green streak of the Yellowstone valley far to the left.

Then Attabury steered his horse beside her once again.

''You should shoot him and bury him,'' she said.

''That's not love.''

''I don't know what you're talking about.''

''I'm talking about walking the extra mile. About doing everything I can, stopping at nothing, to help Con; to give him his chance. I'm in his debt. We all are.''

She said nothing, concentrating on riding through a patch of sage and cedar and gullies.

''I'm the fool who tells the waves to stop and the sun to stand still,'' he said. ''I never could accept my helplessness. When your father took it all away, I couldn't surrender it. He attacked me methodically, with a plan, from all sides at once—courts, piles of lawsuits, publicity in the *Helena Record*. He took the streets. His uglies beat up my men when they left the mine after a ten-hour shift; especially the late shift, in the middle of the night. He even blew up my smelter. I should have surrendered like any sane man. I should have shrugged and packed and left. There's things a man can't fight: he can't fight an invading army. He can't fight an avalanche or a plague of locusts. He can't fight cholera, or consumption eating away his family. I can't do a thing about Con's peritonitis. But here I am, refusing to accept plain reality. I never knew I had that in me. The West did it, I think. God knows, I didn't get so stubborn in Boston.''

"If you expect sympathy from me, you're talking to the wrong person."

"Our future is in your hands."

"You have no future."

"I guess I expected some sympathy."

"You expect sympathy from the woman you kidnapped. Now isn't that clever."

"We've treated you well."

"Abducting me is treating me well?"

"No. But we've been proper with you."

"Proper with me. Should I be grateful?"

"Why, yes. There's right and wrong in this world, and—"

"Right and wrong! Mr. Elwood Attabury, I don't know what you're talking about."

"I'm talking about the things evil men could do to you. Of the wrongs your father did to us—and trying to make it right."

She laughed. "My daddy always says the weak hide behind morality. If they aren't strong enough to win, they make rules."

"The rules were there before your father—and before me, Miss Drogovich."

"Attabury. He gives me whatever I want. He stole your gold mine, and I get what I want."

"Do you have everything you want? Really?"

She didn't, but she wasn't going to confess it to him. She

never had anyone to talk to. She lacked even one friend. No one in the whole world cared about her.

"Of course you don't," he said, answering himself. "How could you? Money won't buy the things people need most. Even the poorest of men can enjoy the things money won't buy. I respect each of these men and they respect me. Luce over there. A dying man. A brilliant manager. Loyal and honest. I'd trust him with everything I possess. Same with Dillingham there. Your father might think everyone has a price—but Angus Dillingham has no price. He couldn't be bought."

"My daddy didn't offer him enough." She was trying to be flippant but didn't succeed. This bandit was unsettling her. "I don't want to hear any more," she added.

"Do you believe in God?" he asked.

She didn't but she refused to say it.

"I do," he said. "And now I'm stricken by my own conscience. I can hardly bear it. I should've let the Fate go; let your father have it. Picked up the pieces and started over. I'm a good geologist and engineer. Not done this. I hurt the innocent. In the end the Divine justice would have worked upon him. But I was in a hurry. I wanted justice right now."

"Will you kindly attend to your bandit duties? I'd like to be alone." She didn't really. Talking—even to this idiot—was better than living with her own thoughts.

"This is my bandit duty, as you put it. You know who we are. Our only chance is for you to see our side of it."

"I'll spare you the effort. No matter what you say, I intend to report you the instant I'm free."

"There. You see? You have ethical feelings after all."

"What are you talking about?"

"You choose to prolong your captivity rather than come to terms. That's very admirable. I admire it in you."

That puzzled her, but not for long. "Mr. Elwood Attabury of Boston, Mass.," she said. "I haven't an ethic or a scruple or an honor or a rule in my head. I do whatever I feel like. You're admiring nothing whatsoever."

"I hoped you might take our side. Now I'll have to keep you. I don't know what to do with you."

"You could return me to my daddy."

"You miss him?"

She sighed. "Do you miss the Fate?"

He laughed. "I think I like you," he said. "You have virtues you're unaware of. Like candor."

Chapter 10

Santiago stood slowly. There were times in life when a man needed more wisdom than he had, and this was one of them. Somewhere within a day's ride, some train robbers were escaping with a fortune in gold bullion and a hostage. If anyone followed, she'd be harmed, they'd told Drogovich. And now Drogovich himself rode westward by rail, Drogovich and his men—and another hostage, his own Mimi. And the message had been the same: don't follow or interfere or she'll be hurt. It seemed the oddest circumstance to him that he stood between a robber gang and another gang led by the victim, and each with a hostage. It looked to be a war among businessmen, and both sides wanted to keep the law out of it. But the law was not out of it; not when murder and robbery were among the crimes.

A wrong step and he might not see Mimi again. Another wrong step and Drogovich might never see his daughter again. He felt, suddenly, a crushing burden. He had to take both threats seriously. The death of the Drogovich woman would haunt him. The death or dishonoring of Mimi would heap grief upon him—and turn him into a different man.

He could stop that special train. Wire Bismarck, demand that the N.P. halt it; wire the sheriff of whatever the county, probably Yellowstone County, to arrest the entire party for abduction. He could do that. And he might never see Mimi alive—and sane—again. Or he could board the westbound in an hour and give chase. He'd have the N.P.'s railroad dicks with him. Three against a large band of plug-uglies.

Too many choices, all of them traps.

Facts, Pericles had said. Get facts. Toole knew that was the next step. He straightened his suit coat and walked into ambush.

"There you are," Mrs. Gatz said. "I thought you'd forgotten me."

"Mrs. Gatz—can it wait?"

"No, it can't. I need to see you right now. And that was an hour ago."

"I'm busy on sheriff business. I'll send for Dr. Hoffmeister—"

"I don't want any schnapps-soaked army surgeon touching me."

"Mrs. Gatz, Fort Keogh is one of the healthiest posts in the West—and it's Dr. Hoffmeister's discipline that did it."

But Mrs. Gatz wasn't listening to him. She parked herself in his rocking chair and opened her mouth. "There," she muttered, a finger jabbing at some offending part of her. "I can't stand it anymore. Hjorts, he says to pull it out because he can't stand *me*."

A tooth. He sighed. Frontier physicians doctored teeth, people, dogs and cats and livestock. "Mrs. Gatz. You have lovely teeth. I wouldn't want to ruin your perfect smile."

"After three babies I should worry about my smile?"

"I'll give you an anodyne today. How about some Dover's Powder? We'll do this some other time."

"No, Hjorts says don't come back until it's out because I'm driving him mad."

"I'll have a look," Santiago said, cursing his own weakness. Reluctantly he peeled off his suit coat, poured water into his washbowl, and scrubbed his hands, wondering what possessed him. He felt like a puppy.

He tilted her back, using a foot on the rocking chair runner, a technique he intended to describe in *Lancet* some day. "Open," he said.

"It's either this one or this one," she mumbled, stabbing at her two lower left premolars.

"Well, which?"

She muttered something. He eyed her lower gum closely, discovering that it was cherry red and swollen in that vicinity.

"I could pull three or four for good measure," he said. "That would narrow it down."

She muttered something unintelligible through the finger stabbing her mouth.

He poked around with a dental pick and found no pulpy spots in the enamel of either. He touched the swollen gum between the base of the teeth and she winced.

"Oh you beast," she muttered.

"Grip the arms of the chair. This'll hurt."

"You're a sadist, Santiago Toole."

"Mrs. Gatz, all doctors love pain. We roll in it like a dog on a dead skunk. We get rich from it. Open wider. That's the way. Don't bite or I'll bite back. How many teeth shall I murder, eh?"

"One!" she cried.

He probed into the swollen area at a likely place that showed signs of laceration. She squirmed. But then he spotted, in the faint light, a shard of something jammed in the gum hard beside a tooth. It resisted the blandishments of his pick, so he rummaged for a dental forceps and snatched at it. Whatever it was—chicken bone, probably—it had wedged into her gum. But after several attempts he plucked it loose.

He mixed some carbolic and water and handed the tumbler to her. "Rinse your mouth and spit it in here," he said.

She did, gagging and drooling.

"Blood! You made it worse. Now I have to come back and you can charge more."

He held the forceps before her with the shard of bone still clamped in its jaws. "This," he said.

"That? I thought you took a tooth. Now you'll say I'm all well."

"It'll be a few days," he muttered.

"Well, I'll go to Dr. Hoffmeister. What's your fee?"

"Oh, fifty cents."

"For that? I hope Hjorts charges double next time you

come in for ten-penny nails or bag balm." She dropped some wooden nickels issued by the bank in his instrument tray.

"I have no use for bag balm," he said. "I don't have bags."

He hastened her out before she could retort to that, and cleaned his pick and forceps in soap and water and then laid them in a pan full of carbolic, remembering the cautions of his surgery instructor, Joseph Lister.

A noble profession, he thought, supplying its mercies to a suffering world.

He donned his suit coat and made his weary way to the N.P. station. He felt oddly alone even there on Main among scores of people he knew—men who'd make up a posse if he asked them. He wouldn't ask. He dreaded taking a posse of amateur deputies to hunt down bandits—and victims—who held hostages against just such a chase. This mess he'd have to resolve on his own. If it could be resolved.

The twelve-thirty westbound would be rolling in soon, and on it would be allies—maybe. Railroad dicks were Napoleons; half of the crime they knew of they hid from sheriffs, the other half they buried. Like the hoboes they accidentally beat to death.

He found Homer Allen, the stationmaster, coffeeing with Varney, the day wire man. Killing time was the true vocation of all stationmasters and telegraphers.

"It's you, Sheriff. We was just wonderin' if you'd gone on a two-week drunk."

"Where'd that special go? The one hired by Drogovich."

"West." He pointed. "West is thataway."

"Homer. You had to clear traffic. Where'd they tell you they were going?"

Homer Allen spat a fine brown streak squarely into a green-crusted brass spittoon. "He wanted the highball, all right. I had to sideline two freights, one through, one local." He grinned. "I thought you was on it. Or was your coppery lady just visitin'?"

"Allen, I need to know fast."

"I heard Bighorn."

"Is there a siding there?"

"Nope. But they was going to git off there. The train, it was to get up to Custer to water and coal up and wait. They wanted the crew to keep steam up and jist set. Good siding there."

Bighorn. The place where a railroad trestle and two ferries crossed wide rivers that could not be forded in June. The place any bunch of westbound robbers would have to come to. The place where Drogovich imprisoned Mimi. The place to which Santiago Toole was forbidden to go. And obviously the place where Drogovich's private army intended to ambush the train robbers and mete out justice—maybe death sentences—well ahead of the law.

"Train robbers," he muttered. "Mostly some mining men."

"Oh, them train robbers knew how to mine," Homer Allen said. "You want to go up there, Sheriff, the N.P.'ll give a pass on my sayso."

The key began chattering and the wireman transcribed. "That was Terry," he announced. "Fifty-six—that's the westbound—just left. She's running an hour slow."

Santiago had an hour and a half. He wondered how to spend it. He pulled the flimsies off the spindle and studied them. Several had to do with the special. Turning it around and clearing track had been a complex operation. The N.P. had run a westbound engine over from Glendive because there was no wye in Miles City to turn one around. Drogovich must have shelled out plenty, he thought.

"You ain't supposed to read them," the wireman said.

He found a wire to Drogovich from Helena: "Whereabouts of Attabury and Luce unknown." Toole folded it and stuffed it in his pocket.

"Hey!" the Western Union man said.

"Evidence," Toole said.

Ten minutes later he slouched in the saddle on his Irish thoroughbred, Saint James, his one luxury, riding toward the trestle over the Tongue River. He eased the leggy horse down a steep embankment, picked up the tracks he'd spotted in the mud, followed them to the point where they vanished into the Tongue, waded across the river on a mucky bottom, and picked them up on the west bank. They led north but vanished where the rain had dissolved them. He found them again under the military bridge, and again on the bank of the Yellowstone where dense cottonwoods had protected the prints. He pulled out his pocket watch and decided he had time for three miles each way. That would take him past Fort Keogh and into some steep river bluffs that crowded the river.

He rode an hour, picking up an occasional print—enough to tell him that the flour-sack bandits had followed the river west. It was something to pursue after he met the railroad dicks.

The hostelry at Bighorn wouldn't let a room to an Indian or breed, and that suited Drogovich fine. For three bits he rented the tackroom of the log horse barn at the rear, and stuffed Mimi in. Better to keep her out of sight anyway. The rest of the log complex suited him fine: it consisted of a saloon and eatery, and three rooms usually rented to passing drummers or drunken cowboys. He took one and rented the others for his eight men, calculating that half of them would be out prowling at any given time.

Various things pleased him. He was glad to escape that bone-jarring immigrant coach. It infused joy in him that a hundred-mile train ride, at the heroic speed of thirty miles of passage in a single hour, had put him and his minions far ahead of Attabury. And it delighted him that his intelligence had won him everything he needed to know: Attabury was not to be found in Helena and neither was Constantine Luce. He knew who he was dealing with and where they were heading. That made matters simple. Even if by some freakish circumstance his quarry slipped through this net, they'd end up back in Helena. But he'd prefer to deal with them here, far from prying eyes. In Helena he'd face constraints, even if he bought and sold judges and sheriffs.

Arnold Carp knew precisely what to do, so Drogovich had stood aside and let him do it. No sooner had the special screeched to a halt than his men had jumped down to the gravel roadbed, there being no station platform. Carp had dispatched one to the Yellowstone ferry, another to the Big Horn River ferry, and a third to the railroad trestle, just in case Attabury had some notion of swimming the horses while his men carried the bullion and booty across the Big Horn on the trestle. Carp sent a fourth and fifth man hiking up the Big Horn in search of any fords that needed watching. The sixth was to unload horses from the boxcar and arrange for their care. The seventh would guard Toole's squaw. The eighth, Carp himself, would keep an eye on the hostelry—just in case.

Drogovich surveyed his rude quarters and decided the first order of business would be bedbugs. He found an old crone in the kitchen rolling Rocky Mountain oysters in batter, and dragooned her into renovating the bedding. The filthy gray blanket was suspect, but not nearly so much as the straw-filled tick he would eventually lower himself onto. Such ticks, especially if they hadn't been washed and the straw renewed, were five-star hotels for bedbugs, with blue-ribbon dining rooms just above.

"I want a fresh tick with fresh straw, and all the rest," he said.

"But sair—"

"Don't but me. Do it or I'll flay your hide."

She scurried out with the tick. Moments later she snatched the straw-filled pillow and the grimy bedclothes as well. He poured tepid water into the cracked washbowl and sluiced railroad cinders and grit out of his eyes and nose and ears. Then he proceeded to a rendezvous with Carp in the saloon, the most amiable of the corners in this squalid place.

Carp had been with him from the beginning and was as reliable as a well-broke dray. Drogovich had paid him badly, but slipped an occasional ounce of gold to the man as an inducement to redouble his efforts. The sallow-fleshed enforcer valued the gifts all out of proportion to their value, which is why Drogovich kept his salary at $6.37 a week.

Together they had planned and executed the assault on the

Fate, with Drogovich handling courts, lawyers, lawmen, and paperwork, while Carp assembled a gang that could dominate the streets and wholesalers and freighters and miners, and intimidate Attabury and his superintendent, Luce.

Attabury's mine lay high up in Oro Fino Gulch above Unionville, and adjacent to the massive holdings of the Whitlatch Mine, which straddled the mother lode that had over eons deposited all the gold in Last Chance Gulch that placer miners had scraped out in the sixties. By the time Attabury had arrived in the Helena district, the Whitlatch was in decline, having lost the gold seam—which yielded about twenty-five dollars a ton—at a fault. They'd bored in all directions but had simply lost the vein. That's when Attabury's geologic genius had come into its own. He'd traced the fault to a point high above Unionville, and had concluded that the vein could be found about a half mile south of where Whitlatch had lost it, and a hundred feet deeper. He'd quietly bought up claims, including a key one from Whitlatch, and then sunk his last penny into a discovery shaft. He had only one chance: he had capital enough to drive the shaft to the proper depth and run some short laterals. It'd been strike gold or bust, and he'd struck it, and named the new mine the Fate in honor of his knife-edged victory.

All that had happened in the seventies, and had renewed the district's production after a time of sharp decline. The Fate had yielded handsomely ever since, producing something like a million and a half dollars' worth of ore over its several years of operation. Attabury's twenty-four-stamp mill crushed the rock, and the free gold was extracted by the mercury amalgamation process in seemingly endless quantities. And that is what had attracted Drogovich in 1882. It had taken two years to drive out Attabury and his cohorts. Carp's street wars had helped, but it wasn't until Drogovich had corrupted the Lewis and Clark County court and sheriff and administrative systems that Drogovich had finally struck it rich. Attabury had crossed no palm with gold, and it'd been his downfall.

Drogovich had taken a certain private pleasure in it. His

Croatian father and Danish mother had arrived in Boston in 1840, along with three-year-old Ingmar, after a stormy Atlantic passage in the bowels of a rotting four-master, and had found there nothing but menial work. The patrician rulers of Boston, all of them with English surnames, had consigned people who spoke a foreign tongue to the lowest employments. His father, Milec Drogovich, had collected and hauled dead horses and cows for a rendering plant; his mother Ingrid had become a domestic, though she'd been born to the merchant class of Copenhagen. Ingmar Drogovich had grown up sharing his parents' loathing of the upper crust—of people like Elwood Attabury III. Unlike his parents, though, he'd done something about it.

"What'll it be, gents?" the saloonman asked, rubbing his hands on a grubby white apron.

"What's your name?" Drogovich asked.

"Why—Axel Vanick. I own it."

"I like to know names. I remember names. Bring us a fresh bottle of Crab Orchard."

The man looked stricken.

"Make it Wilken Family."

"It's opened," Vanick said.

"We'll see," Drogovich said. "Bring water."

"It's all right," Vanick said, eyeing Drogovich's rich attire. "I'll get 'er."

It wasn't red-eye. Drogovich poured shots. Carp preferred his neat, but Drogovich dumped his into a water tumbler and sipped anticipatorily.

"Well, how do you calculate?" he asked.

"Amateurs and packhorses. Tomorrah night at the earliest. They'll try for a night passage through here."

"When do the ferries quit?"

"They don't. You can wake them up if you want one. I just had Murdock check."

"The men'll have to do shifts to keep an eye out."

"I fixed it already."

"How's Toole's squaw?"

"She got a mean look in her eye."

"What'll you do with her?"

"She'll tell no tales. Not to Toole, not to nobody. You just say the word."

"Not yet," Drogovich said. "You never know."

Chapter 11

One of life's minor mysteries for Santiago Toole was just how Myrtle Dillon knew a train was rolling in. He could see nothing as he squinted eastward, peering down the silver rails until they merged on the horizon. But suddenly Myrtle's café crew in the N.P. station had sprung to life and was dishing out plates along the counter and tables of the grubby eatery.

The blackboard announced chicken cordon bleu, but Toole knew it wouldn't be chicken. Most any clement day, Myrtle's lethal son Tommy caught prairie dogs by the score east of town. Myrtle's four-bit special was really fillet of prairie dog smothered in white gravy; mashed potatoes; and a gummy roll served with rather tasty Corona coffee.

Any moment now the café would turn into bedlam as passengers erupted from their coaches for the twenty-minute lunch stop and wolfed food sitting and standing, fearful of the whistle from the hissing Baldwin that would tell them to abandon food or abandon the train. Myrtle offered no options, at least not until everyone who wanted the four-bit plate had been fed. Let a traveler want a glass of water instead of coffee, or griddle cakes instead of chicken cordon bleu, and he'd likely depart hungry.

Her serving ladies, some of them from the sporting district, swooped away dirty dishes and slapped down fresh meals as fast as any seat was vacated, while old Myrtle, hunched froglike over her money box, guarded the portals. Her younger son, lop-eared Willis, was her candy butcher,

hawking peanuts, chocolate confections, cigars, plug tobacco, newspapers, Lash's Bitters, McElree's Cordui, and
box lunches of bread and apples to those who didn't wish to
brave the mobbed counter. Old Myrtle didn't miss a trick,
and knew the needs of what the poets of the railroads called
the congregation of aching spines.

Sure enough, no sooner had the ladies slapped chipped
crockery loaded with prairie dog onto the counters than the
westbound rose out of the horizon and wheezed in, hissing
steam, the engine bell bonging like a national emergency.
The sheriff, with his star pinned to his black suit coat, posi-
tioned himself centrally, hoping to be recognized by men
whose names he didn't know. He thought he could identify
them anyway: railroad dicks wore their profession like an
eight-dollar funeral suit.

Brakemen stood in the opened doorways of the coaches as
they rumbled past, and even before the train screeched to a
halt, they had tossed their step stools to the cinder platform
and stood ready to lend a hand to passengers erupting from
the stinking coaches.

The railroad dicks traveled on a pass, therefore first-class.
Toole spotted them at once, clambering to earth and squint-
ing around in the alarming prairie sunlight like released cons
stepping out of prison. He approached them confidently.

"Gentlemen," he said.

The larger one, fully six and a half feet and axe-handle
wide at the shoulders, scrutinized him as he would a photo-
graph on a dodger, beginning with Toole's black leather shoes
and progressing up his black trousers to his suit coat, dwell-
ing on the steel star, and finally into Toole's smooth-shaven
young face and weary eyes. The shorter one, who didn't top
six feet, accomplished all that with a single dead-eyed glance.

"We use local talent for bit parts," the larger ape said.

"Spear carriers," the other said.

"I have the wrong men, sorry," Toole said, turning away.

"Sheriff."

Toole paused.

"You got the right men."

Toole didn't like it. "Let's talk in the stationmaster's office," he said, and wheeled away. There'd been no handshake, no introductions.

Toole led the dicks into the gloomy office where Homer Allen chewed and spat and watched the mobs on the platform from his grilled window.

"Claghorne," the bigger one said. "Call me Manny."

"Graff Biddle," the shorter one said. "You're Toole."

Santiago nodded. "I'll brief you—after you show me credentials."

Manny laughed but dug into a breast pocket and extracted a ratty leather folder. He flipped it open to reveal a thin badge. Emmanuel Claghorne, Investigator 12, Northern Pacific Railroad Company, it read.

The other one, Biddle, was flapping his badge at Toole as well, and a glance sufficed. Santiago had asked for badges more as a riposte than from any serious doubt.

"All right. I found a trail and want one or both of you with me—if you can ride. The rain almost washed it out."

"You ever been on a horse, Graff?" Manny asked. "I ain't."

"Nope," Graff said. "Never once."

Toole felt relieved. "All right. There's something I'd rather see you do anyway. Get back on this train and take it to Bighorn, a hundred miles from here."

"What's there?"

"A railroad trestle over the Big Horn River; two ferries for road traffic—one across the Big Horn, one across the Yellowstone. The robbers are heading that way as far as anyone knows."

"How do ya know that?"

"The principal suspects live in Helena."

"How do ya know that?"

Santiago ran swiftly through what he knew, ending with Drogovich's army heading that way on the special train. He said nothing about Mimi.

"This heist was some kinda business war?" Manny asked.

"That's my best guess. I'd like you to go there, look like

drummers if you can, keep an eye out. I want the train robbers brought here alive for trial. You'll have to keep Drogovich and his uglies from cheating justice.''

Manny wheezed softly. ''You think him and me''—he gestured toward Graff—''can play drummers? Do sharks play goldfish?''

Toole retreated. No one would ever mistake this pair for traveling salesmen. ''All right. Just go. I have a personal reason. They abducted my wife—with a warning she'd be hurt if I interfered.''

Manny whistled. ''This Drogovich is some fish.''

''His plug-uglies are not vegetarians or Grangers.''

''Ain't this something. The robbers, they got Drogovich's daughter, and Drogovich, he's got your wife. Ring around the rosy. You doin' anything bright?''

Toole had to repress the Irish erupting in him. ''Just go to Bighorn. I need you there.''

''Where you going?''

''I'm following the trail on horseback.''

''You ditching the town?''

''There's Pike Garrison, the town marshal. I deputize him when I'm gone.''

''Get me a horse,'' Manny Claghorne said. ''Graff, you ride the rails.''

''You can't go. You've never been on a horse,'' Toole said.

''Get me a big horse.''

''Look, Claghorne, I don't need a greenhorn on a horse. Tracking is hot, dry, tiring work. We'll be out for days. I can't nursemaid you.''

''Toole, how many of them robbers did you count?''

The railroad dick's argument was impeccable, Toole realized.

The whistle shrieked. Passengers tumbled out of the café, wiping lips, toting greasy rolls.

''Get on and help me. My wife's safety is in your hands,'' Toole said to Biddle.

''What's she look like?''

Toole sucked in air. "She's half French and half Assini-boin—and beautiful."

Biddle laughed. "I'll take a lookee."

"Mr. Biddle, I want those robbers returned here alive. I want my wife kept safe. I'm going to bring Drogovich and his whole party back here—to answer criminal charges. Abduction for one. Impeding the investigation of a crime, for another. Mr. Biddle, I don't expect you to do that alone. Let 'em know the N.P. is watching, that's all. Say nothing about me. Just keep an eye on them and keep Mrs. Toole from harm at all costs. Understand something. You're a private citizen. Don't take the law into your hands. Believe me, I'll prefer charges against anyone that violates the law."

Toole hoped the man heard him. But he sensed that Biddle would end up in Drogovich's little army.

The whistle shrilled twice. Brakemen lifted their step stools.

"Board," the conductor bawled.

"Yeah," Biddle said. "See ya, Manny."

He swung on just as the engine belched dragon claws of steam and the slack slammed out of the couplings.

Toole glared suddenly at Claghorne. "Is he going to play vigilante? My wife's life is in his hands. I love my wife. I'll by God strangle him if she's—"

"You can't expect everything," Claghorne said. "You got a nag big enough?"

"I want you to stay and hold the fort here and handle wires. There's a lot coming in from other lawmen. They want descriptions and all that."

"The livery barn'll have a big horse. I want a mean one. They'll go better than some gentle one."

"Your theories about horseflesh aren't sound, Claghorne. Where're you from did you say?"

"South Chicago."

"That's almost where I'm from," Homer Allen said.

Toole glared. "Homer, everything here's confidential."

"How many of them robbers are there, Toole?" Claghorne asked again.

It was an argument winner. An hour later the railroad dick in the brown checkerboard suit tucked his hightop shoes into the stirrups and grasped the reins of a seventeen-hand dray usually used for pulling light wagons. Toole had put together an outfit for the dude: a slicker and blanket, a shotgun and shells, and some hardtack.

Toole notified One-Word Garrison, the town marshal; stopped at Fort Keogh to ask Adelbert Hoffmeister, the post surgeon, to cover for him; and led Claghorne along the south bank of the Yellowstone, where an occasional hoofprint that survived the deluge enticed them on. Then, a few miles west of Keogh, the tracks disappeared altogether, and Santiago Toole wondered what the hell he was doing there three hours from Miles, along with a railroad dick who winced every time his horse took a step.

It was a matter of race. Always race. Mimi surveyed her prison, lit only by a halo of sunlight around the plank door and a few blinding pinpoints of sun breaking through the chinking of the logs. She found some ratty saddle blankets and spread them on the grimy plank floor for a pallet. Log walls on the outside and thick slabs of rough-sawn plank on the interior wall, along with plank floor and ceiling, comprised her home. A chaotic jumble of ancient saddles, harness, old horseshoes, shoeing nails, bridles, hames, surcingles, and tins of liniment littered the little room. It stank of rats and decaying leather.

Always race. Santiago had made a small sanctuary for her in this white man's world, her father's world, and it was all that stood between her and the rest of Miles City. Her French blood helped not at all. Were it not for his strength and decency, she'd be expelled from the town, with that undertaker, Sylvane Tobias, leading the horsewhip parade. She had it better than her mother, though, up on the Fort Belknap reservation, starving because the buffalo were long gone and the rations distributed by the agent were few. Mimi had sent her a dollar now and then, but she suspected the agent, who distributed the mail, had stolen it.

Always race. Drogovich had thought nothing of abducting a breed woman; it wouldn't even make the newspapers. He knew that. He knew that as a great mining magnate he could do whatever he felt like doing, especially over here in the thinly settled part of the territory.

He'd sat across from her in the third-class coach and asked her multitudes of questions about Santiago. She knew why, and refused to answer in spite of his mounting threats. This Drogovich collected information as a carpenter would collect saws and hammers and planes—to use as handy tools. He wanted to know all about Santo's background; where he was from; how he'd come to Miles; what he earned; whether he ever lost his temper; who his friends were; what he believed; what party he supported. Everything. At first Mimi thought he was just making conversation, and she told him a bit: how Santiago had been the youngest son of an Irish baron at Kilkenny; how younger sons were unwelcome because they could not inherit; how his father had put him through medical school in Scotland and banished him to the New World.

All this Drogovich had devoured with his unblinking stare, until suddenly Mimi had realized that everything she said would only weaken Santo. Santiago would arrest him for this; but a monster like this Drogovich would set his lawyers to work and ruin Santo one way or another. And her too. A cold fear had built in her: in the minds of white men, breeds were supposed to be loose women; Drogovich might have his men use her. And tell the court things that were terrible lies. All to hurt Santo. The thought had evoked tears, which she'd brushed back, not letting Drogovich see her terror and helplessness.

But he had seen. He saw everything, like God.

Now, clapped into a musty room scarcely eight feet square, she faced her dilemma: her life might be over or hopelessly ruined. Outside the door, one of those uglies sat patiently, jailing her. She felt thirst but refused to beg for water. All of this had to do with race. The simple comforts, such as a glass of water when she needed it, or a trip to an outhouse when she needed it, had been taken away, and all because she was

Santiago's wife and had darker flesh and broader cheekbones than her captors. What was the meaning of her life? Was she only a small bit of inferior brown flesh and spirit, a mishap of nature? White men regarded their lives as something sacred and important; they sought to fulfill their every wish and lord it over other white men. But that didn't apply to her. She was only an animal to be caged or killed. On her last trip to Fort Belknap she found them all hollow-eyed, their duties gone, and with them the reasons to live. No longer did a young Assiniboin gather meat or find glory in war and horse stealing. The women no longer decorated their lodges or tried to tan a hide most beautifully, but sat stupidly, sucking booze when they could, frying the white man's flour into greasy cakes to keep the body alive. It would be better if they all were dead! Let her mother's people die away so that the memory of a proud and gifted people might not perish!

She hated white men, even Santo! That thought pierced her, and she sobbed, curled into a ball on the rank blankets. She thought only of night, wanting the protection of darkness. She loved Santo. He had a future even if she had none. She felt grateful that she'd borne no breed children to be persecuted in the full noon of white men's civilization. Even a quarter-blood, as they would be, would be doomed to meaningless drudgery.

And yet there was the mystery: during her girlhood years in the St. Louis convent school where her father had sent her, the sisters had opened her soul. Before her, in the chapel, was an altar devoted to an all-loving God who, they assured her, loved all peoples including the Assiniboin; who came to the desperate and needy to wipe away tears and strengthen the soul and prepare them for the ordeals of life; who, if she believed, would give her grace and the promise of paradise in the next world if not this sorry one.

She remembered that. And she thought of Ingmar Drogovich, and then those plug-uglies of his. Her mother's people all believed in the spirits; not very many white men believed in anything. That was the trouble. The sisters had taught her the great rule: do unto others as you would like others to do unto you. Love thy neighbor. But so few of the whites bothered to heed it. Instead, they called her mother's people heathen, and that was the excuse to cheat them, starve them, steal their land. The agent sent to protect them had given them some mean part of their government rations—and sold the rest. He lived in a great house behind a white picket fence. Behind the house was a coop full of fat chickens, a barn full of fat cattle, and a great garden. Her mother's people were forbidden to pass the fence, so they stood in front by the hour and day, and stared at the chickens and cattle.

She lay quietly in the gloomy heat as the last of the day slid by. She felt parched, but had turned stoic like her mother's people, and harshly commanded her body to wait. She could tell by the fading light and cooler air that much of the June evening had slid by. She wished she could pray, but her supplications caught in her throat. Maybe she could at night; to pray was to cast helplessness aside and clutch at hope.

Was there escape? She slid around the floor looking for a loose plank. And then the walls. She found nothing helpful. She pushed on a ceiling plank and found it firmly anchored. She tried the others. All nailed tight. She examined the tools at hand—hammers, rasps, nippers, a crowbar—and knew she could eventually pry her way free if she were not guarded.

Defeated, she settled into her pallet again, resignation seeping into her. They had penned her body but not her soul and spirit. In her mind's eye she flew over her mother's earth like a great eagle wheeling. She weighed the things that might happen to her and came to a decision. She still had a few choices. Whatever she did, whatever she chose to say, she'd do for Santiago. That would be her gift to him: life had all compressed down to that. She'd give up herself for the man she loved.

That's when she heard voices outside and the tread of feet.

Chapter 12

The horses were giving out, and the long June evening was fading at last. Elwood Attabury III looked for a place to hole up. They'd paralleled the Yellowstone but well north of it, across bleak prairie broken by shallow coulees that drained into the distant river. One place was as good as another because the storm had left water standing everywhere. He settled on a grassy plateau within the jaws of a coulee and nodded to his colleagues.

"We'll rest awhile," he said.

He ached for tea, but there'd be none. Not a stick of wood was to be had, and the buffalo chips were soaked.

Wearily, his men dismounted. Dillingham helped Luce down and then settled a blanket over the wounded man. Ferrero and Astleheim unloaded the horses, dragging the heavy sachels of gold into a central pile, while Chico watered and picketed the horses, which began ripping grass out by the roots in their greed.

Elwood watched the Drogovich woman vanish around a shoulder. "Two minutes," he yelled. She ignored him. He intended to keep a sharp eye on her lest she slip away in the night.

He knelt beside Con and slid a palm over his forehead. Feverish. Con stared back from eyes with black circles under them. A gray pallor had risen in his flesh.

"Taking me along isn't doing me any favor, Elwood," he whispered.

"Where there's life there's hope, Con."

"This stuff"—he waggled the hand that gripped the blue bottle—"this stuff masks it. It'll be gone soon. Going down below, too. Shot a good man. Isn't much that the Maker can do but ship me out. I could use a sip of water."

Dillingham lifted Luce up, and Attabury pressed a canteen to the man's lips. Luce drank only a few sips.

"I shouldn't have started this," Attabury said.

"No, you shouldn't," Luce muttered. "But she's done. And now you gotta do what's needful. Can't retract it. I can't catch those bullets I fired. So go on, go on into the future. It can't be taken back and erased."

Attabury stood slowly, admiring Luce. The dying was urging life upon the living. Go on, go on, make what you can of it. Don't wallow in guilt; get on with living.

"You're an inspiration, Con," he said.

"I'm an opium fiend," Luce retorted, wheezing a little.

Attabury felt the ache in his limbs from a night and day of riding. He could ride passably, but it had gone worse for Dillingham, Ferrero, and Astleheim, who'd scarcely been on a saddle horse in their lives. That was part of the reason these nags were badly used. Deadweight like gold exhausted a horse, but even worse was an inexperienced rider bouncing and resisting the natural movement of the animal. Horse and rider both suffered when that happened.

Filomena Drogovich reappeared, striding easily, her skirt whirling and her brassy hair catching the last light and holding it like a lantern. Elwood had a feeling that she was a middle-European goddess, lithe and glowing, with her porcelain complexion ruddy from the day out of doors.

"There, your biggest problem has returned," she said. "I suppose you have filet mignons and sauteed onions ready."

"Hardtack. No wood even for tea."

"Well, one can't expect much from train robbers."

It hurt. Somehow, Elwood didn't consider himself a train robber. He and his colleagues were only restoring what had been stolen. He wasn't an outlaw; he was an upright man from an upright family, a man with a profession. He wasn't one of those patricians clustered along Beacon Street and the common, with shipping companies and textile mills in their back pockets, or living in splendor around the Back Bay. But his family was old and upstanding and solid. Elwood Attabury the first and second were barristers. He'd attended Roxbury Latin School. His cultivated parents had steered him toward the Boston Athenaeum and reminded him that he lived in the Athens of America. But science had drawn him from that other world. No. Each day he'd crossed the Charles River and gulped down geology and engineering and physics and chemistry at the new Institute of Technology—and now he was a train robber.

"You're very beautiful," he said, startling both himself and her.

"I think so too," she said. "But I'm an unavailable prize. I tell them I'm destined for an arranged marriage to a rich man."

"Surely young men have noticed."

"Old men notice it more and have fewer scruples."

"I wish I might have met you in another time and place."

"I wish I'd never met you at all."

He found himself gazing at her raptly. Something about her gathered light and held it there in the lavender twilight. Maybe it was the kinked brass of her hair. Or the alabaster of her cheeks. Whatever it was, she glowed, and an inexpressible yearning seared through him. A train robber.

"Well, stop staring. I wish to be fed. And what are you going to do with me?"

Dillingham handed her three hardtack rolls. She bit into them lustily, as if they were bonbons.

"I don't know," Elwood muttered.

"Some leader you are," she snapped between chews. "I'll tell you what to do: you don't want to release me because I'll yell bloody murder and name names the moment I'm freed. So you have to hold on to me, right?" She waited for him to agree.

"Right," he said.

"So you divide up. You should give the gold to these poor idiots you roped into this—whatever their share. And tell

them to beat it. Go somewhere. Arizona, Sandwich Islands,
Argentina. Maybe they have to slip into Helena first, get their
families. They're safe as long as you hold me; no one knows
who you are—except me. After they're all gone, you can
release me.''

It was a good plan—the only plan, he thought. But
why . . .

"You have some scheme of your own you're trying on
me.''

"Nope. I'm just smart. If you can't figure what to do, then
you need help.'' Something mirthful lit her eyes and made
her all the more ravishing to him.

"I'll think about it.''

"Some bandit leader you are. Thinking about it. Let them
save themselves. Or do you want them all to be hanged like
you?''

Odd, but he hadn't thought about hanging before. A noose
around his own pale neck. Something convulsed in his stomach. He hadn't shot the expressman, but he'd been there.
He'd be as guilty as Con in the eyes of the law.

The others sat on the bunchgrass chewing on their biscuits
and listening to all this. Elwood knew they were all innocents, good men he'd talked into something shady. Poor Dillingham had been a rock of integrity—and now was a train
robber. Chico, the Welsh miner, had come simply because
Drogovich's uglies had broken his left arm and hand in four
places, rendering him useless in the mines, robbing him of
a living. Ferrero had been pounded senseless for sticking
with Attabury and could find no work in the district. Only
Astleheim had no great personal grievance. Oh, Drogovich
had kept him out of work too, but he could work elsewhere.
A good powder man was always in demand. But Astleheim
had an angry, honed and razored sense of justice, and joined
Attabury's party just to see the world made right again—at
least a little bit.

Elwood Attabury knew, then, what he'd do. He rose
slowly, dusted dead grass off his britches, and approached
his men. "You heard her. I agree with her. Only I'm going

to go further. I'm giving everything to you. I don't want any of it. I'm sick of it. I couldn't look at it without being sick of it. But you earned it. You and Con Luce. I'll save out a share for him—for his family. We'll rest here for a while. Before dawn we'll parcel it out. Each of you—get going. Think about a place now. Some place a long ways away. I can hold her for a week or two, take care of Con too. I'll just hole up when we get to the Musselshell. That's empty country. You'll have time to get away. You'll all be a thousand miles from the territory with enough to start a new life if I hold her.''

They peered into the ground as if the grass before their eyes was the source of divine wisdom. Elwood knew it was actually the first time they had felt the chill reality of being fugitives.

Con Luce looked to be asleep, huddled under his blanket, but it was he who raised an objection. ''Elwood, nah. She's got her own plan. After they leave, and there's only you and my corpse, she's going to give you the slip.''

That hadn't occurred to him.

''That's a possibility,'' she said. ''I would probably succeed. Amateur bandits aren't much good at keeping someone prisoner.''

''Leave it to the opium fiend,'' Luce muttered.

''Do you think that if you don't take your share you're freed of guilt?'' asked Angus Dillingham.

Elwood had thought just that.

''We're in this together,'' Astleheim said.

''My daddy'll catch you.''

Enrico Ferrero pointed at Elwood. ''I done it for him, not me. He got robbed bad. Not many get millions stole right out from under.''

Elwood saw how it was going and knew how it'd end. They would all stick together. They'd insist that Elwood keep the largest share of the bullion. They wouldn't flee in every direction. They'd done this not just to compensate themselves, but for something larger and more noble that lifted it above thievery.

"What a pack of amateurs," Filomena said. "My daddy'll eat you alive." She sounded as if she was cross at them.

Slowly Santiago retraced their steps, looking for the subtle impression in rain-dimpled clay that would signal that he'd found the robber trail again. Manny Claghorne followed like a Saint Bernard on a Shetland pony, contributing nothing. He lacked the eye, he had said. Santiago cut from the river-bank inland to the foot of the bluffs, and found nothing. He backtracked and tried it again, finding only fresh prints of a coyote. He retreated again until he'd gone almost a mile back toward Miles City, where at last he picked up some faint prints. There he circled, found nothing. He stopped, puzzled, defeat blossoming in him.

"What'd they do? Fly?" Manny asked. His cigar bobbed as he talked. "I don't believe in no miracles. You think mebbe they hopped a freight? Like a buncha bindlestiffs? I trown a few hundred of them off the cars."

Toole grunted. The N.P. rails did run through there, hemmed close to the river by the bluffs. But his thoughts had drifted back to his medical college days and an anatomy lecture by a surgeon at Glasgow Hospital, Leverett Case. "If ye don't know for sure where ta cut," Dr. Case had said, "don't ye cut. Get a man who does know where to cut and what lies under. If ye don't know, get an expert, eh? It's only your patient's life at stake."

"Manny, we've got to start over," Toole said. "I'm a doctor—not a tracker. I know a man in Miles that can track an ant. He can see the prints of a spider. Old frontiersman. If he's sober . . ." Toole muttered.

"You mean we gotta ride back?"

"You see any trail?"

"They're bindlestiffs. They hopped a freight."

"With horses? Or did they all ride Pegasus?"

"Who's that? Some derby winner?"

"A mythic flying horse. He carried Bellerophon in his attack on the Chimera."

Claghorne's cigar flapped dangerously. "Yer some sheriff, Toole."

Defeated, Toole turned back in the late light of the June evening, his mind crowded with worries about Mimi.

"What kind of man is Graff Biddle?" he asked.

"Him? He'd as soon knock heads as think. Perfect for the old N.P. I seen him clean out a gondola of tramps in three minutes flat."

"What does he think of Indians?"

"Him? He don't think. He don't like them a bit. Onct one tried liftin' his black Irish hair, so Graff, he throws him in the river. They were on a trestle. Rivers are something. They're God's gift to railroad dicks. You got a froze-up bindlestiff, you stuff him under the ice. That way the law don't get involved. Like you. We bring some bindlestiff to you, and you'd have to get a report and file charges and all that."

"Not in my county, you don't. You bring them to me."

"How come?"

"It's the law. And I'm a doctor. Maybe they're still alive and I can help. And—all mortals are God's children and ought to be buried with respect."

"You some religious frantic?"

"No, I'm a misplaced Irishman." Santiago sighed. He wished he'd followed Drogovich to Bighorn and left the dicks in Milestown.

"I wanna get off," Claghorne said. "This saddle ain't made right."

"Hang on for twenty minutes."

"They don't know how to make saddles here."

They rode in at dusk, rattling over the military bridge and onto Main Street. Toole rode straight toward a slouching southside saloon on Park Street. A sun-bleached sign proclaimed Red Ward's Vaudeville House.

"Where's this?" Claghorne asked.

"The home of Chief Sliding Mountain."

"Some Injun chief?"

"He makes out to be. He's actually half Mexican and half something else. Maybe Corsican or Filipino."

"What's he do?" Claghorne was avalanching off his livery barn horse, which sidestepped and jerked at the reins.

"He plays Chief Sliding Mountain. In the massacre scene."

They tied up the nags and plunged through batwing doors into a wall of stale-beer air. Toole spotted his man in the far corner hunkered into the plank walls, a brace of revolvers on the table before him. That meant Toole was too late. But it was worth trying, anyway.

"Bronco," he said.

The man peered up, surveyed the sheriff and Claghorne, lifted his revolver and shot Toole in the heart. Toole felt the wad pop his badge. Three customers cheered and clapped.

"Yaar," Claghorne yelled, a spring-released shoulder-holster gat filling his hand.

"Don't!" Toole cried, deflecting Claghorne's hand upward. A roar smacked out, followed by missiles of splintered ceiling plank. "It's a stage gun. Just blanks."

"I should kill 'im anyway, dumb stunt like that. I've done it for less."

"Bronco's the best tracker I know."

A barmaid appeared. "Yeah, you should see where his hands track," she said. "Right here." She pointed. Claghorne gaped.

"I need you, Bronco," Toole said.

"Tonight?"

"Now."

"Is there a moon?"

"Not yet."

"All right," he said. "I can sniff it. The usual?"

"The usual." Payment would be one bottle of red-eye.

"Now," Bronco said.

"Later."

"Now or forget it."

Toole feared it was too late after all. "All right. Now. But I'll carry it for a while."

"Hit him on his bean," Manny said. "We'll kidnap him. A brakeman's stick works nice."

By the time they'd gotten Bronco outfitted and aboard a horse, a moon had slinked over the eastern hills. Wearily Toole led them westward again past a dark Fort Keogh and into an area where the bluffs narrowed the river bottoms.

Toole reined up. "All right, Bronco," he said.

The sheriff and Claghorne waited while the wiry little man padded about on foot, occasionally bending close to the clay to study a faint print. He looked like a hound tracking a fox into its den. He pushed through brush, circled the base of the bluffs, and vanished.

"How come he can see in the dark?" Claghorne asked.

"He's not seeing. It's some sixth sense he's got. He's better than a bloodhound."

"I don't believe it. Say, they didn't make this saddle right. Mind if I step off?"

But Bronco returned and wordlessly clambered onto his nag and rode back a ways. The helpless spectators followed. Bronco slid off lithely and plunged into his dog circles again, this time spiraling close to the riverbank. Then he paused, a dim figure beside the water.

"Aar," he said.

Toole on his mount and Claghorne on foot crashed through willow and chokecherry brush and discovered a small meadow beside the riverbank. And on it, an overturned rowboat.

"They took," Bronco said. He turned the rowboat over, exposing a pair of oars. And he pointed at some hoofprints directly under the boat. All around them, now that Toole studied the place, he found trampled grass and shrubbery, broken stems and gouged earth. The rain had blurred the prints, but the turmoil remained.

Beside them the river ran black and swift like a torrent of oil, its far bank barely visible in the pale light.

"You mean they rowed over?"

"Yup," Bronco said.

"Swam the horses? But it's too swift."

Bronco laughed. "Them damn good professional river walkers."

"But that current would've put them a half mile downstream."

"You find them tracks on the other side."

Maybe they did, Toole thought. Maybe some exceptionally powerful men rowed the gold and supplies over and then themselves, and some genius with horses swam them even in that murderous deluge. He knew he'd have to look. He eyed Claghorne skeptically and knew he'd not attempt a crossing with him. They'd have to go back to Miles and wake up the ferryman and get him to unlock his ferry and cross them in his cable-guyed barge.

The robbers had crossed to the north bank. They'd done not just the improbable, but the impossible. Toole grudgingly admired bandits with skills like that.

He surveyed his army: Bronco and Claghorne, one half soused, the other helpless on a horse. It'd have to do. With any luck, he'd have his robbers before Drogovich heard a word of it.

Chapter 13

The one called Carp led Mimi through the darkened rear door into a corridor and then into Drogovich's room. The sole kerosene lamp revealed her leonine captor standing at the window looking faintly amused. Slabs of beef and some small boiled potatoes lay on a platter. A battered knife and fork rested beside a chipped plate.

Carp retreated and closed the door behind him.

"Eat," Drogovich said.

She sat and began while he watched. She hoped he would remain silent. She found the gray meat tasteless, but the small potatoes were edible. This rude place had provided no seasoning and no napkins. She ignored his stare and would not meet his probing gaze. She didn't know what the next minutes would bring, but if he intended to have his way with her, she wasn't going to cooperate.

"The food is bad," he said. "I had some earlier."

She ignored him. Why speak to one who had taken away her liberty?

"My men are out watching the ferries and trestle. The earliest Attabury could get here is about dawn. But tomorrow afternoon would be more likely."

She didn't know who Attabury was. Drogovich seemed to know who had robbed the train. The meat felt good in her stomach and swept away the gnawing hunger and her faintness. She drank a tumbler of water and poured more from a blue-speckled metal pitcher. She devoured everything there was to eat and then sat quietly.

121

"Tell me about yourself," he said. "I suppose people of mixed blood face a difficult life."

"If you are going to have your way with me, do it. Don't expect me to cooperate."

He laughed softly. "You think that Drogovich is an evil man," he said. "So does Drogovich. He's thought much about sin and greed. Life is a trap."

"Why do you speak of yourself that way? Like talking about another person?"

"So I can watch myself."

"I wish to be taken to the barn now."

"We'll talk. You didn't answer the question."

The power of his gaze mesmerized her. He seemed to be able to see right inside of her with those burning gray eyes. She found herself wanting to talk, but she wouldn't.

"Drogovich wishes to learn about Toole. Will he be foolish and come with a posse?"

"I won't talk about him. I will not betray him."

Drogovich abandoned the window and sat down opposite her, too close. The yellow light of the lantern on a sideboard illumined one half of his face. "For you, a mixed-blood, Toole is an island," he said. "You're safe on his island. You're not starving with your mother's people on the Fort Belknap reserve. You're not unwelcome among white men in Miles. You adore him. I see it in your face."

He utterly startled her. How could he read her so well? She had clung to Santo with desperation and love, and indeed he was her island, her only refuge. "Why are you saying this?" she asked.

"Drogovich's success in life is based on fathoming people."

"I don't wish to talk," she said. In truth she couldn't fathom him at all. Perhaps he was merely lonely and wanted female company. She would give him nothing. But she'd listen if she had to. Maybe she'd learn something.

"Of course you don't. You're like a sparrow in a cage. You fear you'll say something that would harm your husband. You have a good husband. Toole's a conscientious man; a good doctor with a mission. He didn't hesitate to help a wounded robber. Even if it was a robber he'd hang later. His Hippocratic oath means something to him. Drogovich admires men like that. Their whole universe has meaning and order in it."

He was trying to draw her out. Especially about Santo. She sat grimly.

"Toole is a better man than Drogovich."

It startled her. She listened intently.

"Drogovich stole a mine. The owner was Attabury. All this"—he waved a ring-studded hand in an arc—"is revenge and restitution. Drogovich took the Fate from Attabury. Drogovich sank him with lawsuits. Bought judges. Scared off his help. Finally it fell to him by way of a judgment. The judge agreed that the vein apexed in Drogovich's half acre and he had a right to the vein. That's mining law, you know. There's now a rich judge in Helena. And a rich sheriff. And several rich lawyers. And some rich county commissioners. But Attabury struck back. A fool's mission, but understandable. Drogovich understands Attabury and admires him. He's salty."

"Don't talk about yourself as a separate person."

Drogovich smiled. "It's a way I have. I'm fascinated by this man Drogovich."

"Which one am I talking to?"

"There is only one."

"Why are you talking to me? Why am I here?"

"Confession. You'll be Drogovich's confessor. We all need that, eh? Especially one who does great evil. The worse one behaves, the more one needs a confessor."

Confession. "You are talking to the wrong person."

"No, you'll do splendidly."

"I wish to leave."

"A confessor is bound to secrecy. Drogovich's confessed much."

She found herself trembling, swimming in currents that threatened to suck her under. "Mr. Drogovich, anything you tell me I'll tell Santo. Anything you tell me'll be evidence against you. I won't keep your secrets. I won't help you. You've abducted me. I'm a captive woman. I'm not some—some priest. Or medicine woman."

"It's a pity."

The way he said it shot a chill straight through her. It was as if she'd heard her death sentence. She felt tears rise in her eyes and fought them back. She lifted her fingers to her ears and felt her pulse ringing in her head. But her fingers kept out nothing.

"Ingmar Drogovich lives in a brand-new brick mansion on the hill above Last Chance Gulch," he said. "Beside him are the great merchants and gold kings of the territory. He joined them when he stole the Fate. He went to their parties and invited them to his. He laughed at poor Attabury, who moved from the hill because he no longer had the Fate. Attabury named it well—the Fate. What a name for a bonanza. It was his fate and now it's mine. And I sit in my study and peer down over the city. And I know I need a confessor."

He'd stopped referring to himself as someone else. She pulled her fingers from her ears and listened. She knew, with aching certainty, that each word of his confession would be a nail in her coffin. She knew why he'd selected a mixed-blood; someone of no account in the territory; someone unknown and unnoticed. She knew her own fate as a vessel for an evil man's guilt. He'd pour his guilt into her until she held it all—and then bury his guilt. And she'd know when he was done: he'd no longer be talking of himself as another person.

"My parents would grieve for me if they knew how Ingmar turned out. They sailed over here when I was a tiny child. They landed in Boston and did menial things because they spoke strange tongues and had to. They both worked hard for Ingmar, built up a little nest egg in the New World—until they died from being all worn out. Ingmar took the money and thought they were fools. The wealthy Yankees had only scorned the peasants. Ingmar would live a better life, eh? He did. But he discovered the ghosts of his mother and father peering at him. All the time, over his shoulder.

And they are saying, 'There's no shortcuts. There's good and evil, right and wrong.' ''

Mimi would not meet his gaze. She tried not to listen but couldn't help it. He spoke almost in a whisper, but each word haunted her and carried with it the seed of her doom.

"Ah! I see terror in you. Drogovich misses nothing. A confession is a dangerous thing to the one who hears it.''

"Have mercy, Mr. Drogovich. Let me go now. I only want to curl up in the barn. I don't want to hear about your sins.''

"That's not your fate. It's not the past you'll hear about, but the future. Poor Drogovich. The man suffered much, you know. Every time his bullyboys struck, some humble miner very like his own father was wounded. Or his small pay, a few bills in a brown envelope, was taken. And some poor woman very like Drogovich's mother would face a week without a few coins for food and clothing for her children. And some of those men, so much like Drogovich's father— they'd been too battered to work again. But Drogovich never stopped. He tried to buy the Fate's accountant to get at the books and rig them and cheat Attabury, but the accountant was a good man—better than . . . I'll ever be. So he burnt the man's cottage and left a sign. But Drogovich hasn't taken lives—he stopped short of that because not even bought judges and sheriffs and newspapers could keep him out of trouble.''

"Please don't talk of yourself as someone else.''

"Very well. I won't. My scruples kept me from finishing the job, but no longer. And not here where there's no law. We're going to capture Attabury and his men and take them where they'll never be found. Maybe Tierra del Fuego, the southern tip of Chile. No one'll ever know—except for you. There'll be no proof of anything. No proof that Attabury ever came this way. Your poor Toole might suspect—but he'll never know.''

That was the most terrifying thing he'd said to her. She read her fate in it and felt a leaden despair crowd her heart.

"There. I've confessed. I've told you my plans. You're a

part of it now. And you wonder what Fate has in store for you.''

''I already know.''

''No you don't know. You don't know anything. You're my scapegoat. You don't know what a scapegoat is. Do you?''

She shook her head woodenly.

''Ah. You need education. A scapegoat's in the scriptures.''

''You're talking about the Lamb of God. And blood sacrifice.''

He laughed harshly. ''See where ignorance gets you. I read. All my life I conquer ignorance. How can one get ahead by knowing little? I'll read to you and then you'll know what a scapegoat is.''

He dug within a portmanteau and extracted a Bible. He sidled toward the little yellow flame in its glass chimney.

''Leviticus,'' he said. ''Ah, here, here. You should know these things.

''And when he hath made an end of reconciling the holy place, and the tabernacle of the congregation, and the altar, he shall bring the live goat.

''And Aaron shall lay both his hands upon the head of the live goat, and confess over him all the iniquities of the children of Israel, and all their transgressions in all their sins, putting them on the head of the goat, and shall send him away by the hand of a fit man into the wilderness:

''And the goat shall bear upon him all their iniquities unto a land not inhabited: and he shall let go the goat in the wilderness.''

He stopped reading and restored his Bible to his luggage.

She wondered what wilderness she would inhabit and what burdens had been laid on her. And whether she'd ever see Santo again. ''*Mon Dieu!* You think I'm the scapegoat! You think you can put your sins onto me!''

An odd joy filtered into his face. ''I've done it several times. When my burdens become too heavy. It restores me.''

"It's not repentance."

"It's as close as I can come."

"And just where is the wilderness I'm to go to?"

"The Sandwich Islands. They'll like a mixed-blood in the houses."

She stared at him in horror.

Drogovich smiled. "Carp'll take you back," he said.

Once again Santiago Toole found himself in Miles City. He'd been over forty-eight hours without sleep and could barely navigate his horse.

"Claghorne, we'll start at dawn."

"You ain't gonna wake up the ferry man?"

"Do you see any moon?"

"Nope."

"We could cross now and shiver through the night over there waiting for light."

"I gotcha."

Bronco said, "You don't need me no more. I'm cutting."

"I do need you—at dawn. You're the tracker."

"Nah. I need a hangover."

The logic of that eluded Santiago. "Meet me in the morning. Put the horse in the livery barn. The ferry at dawn."

Bronco didn't answer but rode into the blackness.

"I'm going to Macqueen House. The N.P. pays," Claghorne said.

"Dawn," Toole said. "Before dawn if you can."

Claghorne avalanched off his giant horse and led it away.

Some posse, Toole thought. He made his way by starlight to his cottage, which loomed bleakly out of the night. He put Saint James away in the inky barn, taking care to rub the Irish thoroughbred and grain it.

He stumbled into his kitchen and made his way to his bedroom, feeling the desolation. The room without Mimi was as cold as a prison cell. He collapsed on the bed, thinking to plan the next day's attack—but the next thing he knew, the sun pummeled his eyes. He startled into full awareness, realizing at once that dawn had come and gone. His head throbbed. He rubbed the bristles of his beard and clambered off the bed. The hands of the pocket watch in his waistcoat had navigated past ten o'clock. Mindlessly he wound it. Some sheriff he turned out to be.

A few minutes later he found Claghorne sitting on grass near the ferry landing, holding the reins of his livery nag.

"Dawn," Claghorne said.

Toole nodded. There was nothing to say. They boarded the barge, leading their horses, while old Erastus squinted at them malevolently. Santiago had always thought that Erastus was the only ferryman alive who hated business.

"That's four-bits a horse and two-bits a man," he said.

"Bill the county."

"Bill the county! Bill the county! Raise our taxes! It takes me forever to get it from the county!"

Nonetheless, he eased the scow off the landing. The guy wire was strung at an angle to let the river current do the work in this direction, and swiftly the slapping current shoved the barge to the north bank, where it ground to a stop.

It took Claghorne three leaps to throw a leg over his nag, but eventually he managed, except he lost his derby on the third lurch. Toole collected it for him.

"You ready to ride?" Toole asked maliciously.

"Dawn," Claghorne retorted.

Santiago led them west along the bank, keeping a close watch for tracks. He found a few rain-blurred ones downstream from the rowboat on the far shore. A day's summer sun had dried the mud, preserving the evidence. Toole felt no joy. He and a railroad detective who'd be too saddlesore to go far would tackle a band of murderous desperadoes—if they could ever catch up.

"Claghorne, you're going to slow me down. Why don't you go back? Just stay in Miles and keep the lid on."

"I'm coming."

"You won't last another hour."

"You need firepower."

Toole laughed. "Firepower. Against a gang?"

Claghorne remained expressionless.

"All right. You can quit any time and find your way back. I can't take you back." Toole steered Saint James along the elusive trail up the river, through open flats and occasional timbered areas where cottontails and willows offered shade. It felt good to be on a trail, even an old one. He slouched into his saddle and let himself sway to the rhythm of the big horse. He rode that way into the afternoon, paying no attention to the man behind him.

"You mind if I get off?" Claghorne asked.

Toole stopped and waited.

"Help me off. I can't make my leg go over."

"You'd better go back, Claghorne. You're a railway detective, not a posse man."

Claghorne avalanched off the nag. It sidestepped, yanked free. Claghorne tumbled into grass like a lung-shot buffalo. Toole turned Saint James and snatched the trailing reins of the giant livery gelding.

"Holy mackerel," Manny Claghorne said. Slowly he clambered to his feet and managed a few wooden steps.

"Where'd you learn that rough language?" Toole asked.

"The N.P., it docks us if we swear. Bad for the business."

"Look, Claghorne, at this rate they're gaining on us every hour. You'd better go back."

"I can't," he said helplessly. "I'll just walk behind you. Walking'll fix me up. I got some lumbago of the knees."

Santiago shrugged and heeled the thoroughbred. It took off in a brisk walk. Claghorne lumbered along behind, losing ground, sweating and muttering.

"Toole!" he yelled from fifty yards back.

Sighing, Toole turned around. His every instinct was to ditch Claghorne. But the doctor within him knew that Claghorne couldn't go either direction; couldn't board his nag; couldn't do anything. To leave him behind was to endanger his life from exposure.

He found Claghorne curled up in the grass, hanging on to the reins of his nag. Great drops of sweat had collected on the man's forehead.

"I can toss bindlestiffs off a car, the more the merrier. I

can kidney-punch some drunk. I can wallop a brakeman and beat him with his own stick. I can pull out my piece faster than a three-card monte swindler on a Pullman.''

Santiago dismounted and tied Saint James's reins to a thick juniper. Then he dug into his sparse medical kit. He didn't have laudanum but he had Dover's Powder in two-grain capsules.

''Where do you hurt?'' he said, but he already knew.

Claghorne laughed dourly.

''You have any illnesses I don't know about? Heart trouble?''

''Not until today.''

''I've an anodyne. I'll get some water.'' Toole unscrewed the cup top from his canteen and dipped it into the cold water of the Yellowstone. ''All right, take this.''

''What's that?''

''An opiate.''

''Yeah? You gonna turn me into a fiend?''

''It's that or sit here for a day until you can walk. And then walk ten miles back.''

''That far, is it?''

Toole didn't answer. He was feeling testier by the moment.

''All right. But I'll tell them you forced me to.'' Claghorne snatched the capsule and the cup and did the deed.

''It's fast. It'll take a few minutes. Then I'll take you back.''

Toole sat in the grass watching Claghorne. The man sat expectantly, as if waiting for a trip through the pearly gates. Then Claghorne stood. He smiled. He walked tentatively. Then he strutted. Then he swung up on his nag.

''Let's go git them devils,'' he said.

''Claghorne, I'm taking you back. I don't have enough Dover's Powder to float you for a week, much less two or three—which it may take.''

''Toole—don't say that to old Manny.''

Sighing, Toole swung up on his horse and started toward Miles, feeling as if a cloud had blotted all the sun from his life. Manny didn't follow. Toole waited. Manny turned west and steered up the trail of prints cast in mud like concrete.

Toole had a choice, and made it. He turned his horse west.

Chapter 14

Elwood posted a guard that night not because he believed anyone was on their trail, but to keep Filomena from stealing a horse and sneaking away. There were enough of them to do it in two-hour watches. At dusk he'd studied their backtrail from a high point with his field telescope and seen nothing. He didn't expect to. No one would believe they'd crossed the swollen Yellowstone.

But Filomena slept soundly under a blanket he'd given her. She seemed as tired as the rest of them, and settled down after a few tart remarks about the mattress of bunchgrass she was lying on. Elwood rested uneasily, his conscience working on him like a dripping faucet. It seemed a long night; the longest he'd known, haunted as he was by the ruin of his life. He'd taken the last watch and saw the eastern horizon turn gray about five in the morning.

When the light permitted, he knelt beside Con Luce and slid a hand to the injured man's forehead. Luce barely stirred, but finally his eyes flickered open. "Burning up," he whispered.

"You'll make it, Con. Hang on. In a day or two we can hole up and let you rest. You'll get past this. I just know it."

"Thirsty.

Elwood propped Luce up and let him sip water. The others stirred. Filomena threw her blanket off and vanished behind a shoulder of land. Chico undid hobbles and began saddling horses. Dillingham passed out more biscuits of hardtack. Filomena returned, and even in that somber gray her brass

132

hair caught light and held it. Her beauty melted Elwood Attabury's soul. How could he have abducted someone so lovely?

"Well?" she said. "I don't want hardtack for breakfast."

Dillingham handed her several pieces.

"Thank you. You're so thoughtful."

"We can't risk a fire now. Later. Tonight we'll cook."

"You'll cook all right," she retorted.

Ferrero brought her horse, and she hiked her skirts and clambered up. Those calves dizzied Elwood. She knew it and hiked her skirts again to her knee. Then she smiled. "It's not for train robbers," she said. "Too bad for you."

"Too bad for me," Elwood echoed.

They lifted Con Luce up in front of Dillingham again. Luce had lost a lot of ground in the night and had become delirious.

"Need the juice," he muttered. "It hurts."

Luce could no longer lift the bottle of laudanum to his lips. Elwood did it, shocked at how much the man had consumed in such a short time. A normal dose was five drops. The bottle was down an inch.

"I'm a dope fiend," Luce muttered.

Dillingham shook his head and propped Luce up.

They rode out silently, each aware that Con Luce had slipped badly in the night. Elwood wondered if Luce would last the day, especially when the heat built up late in the afternoon. He wondered how to bury Luce; he had no shovel. They hadn't planned on anything like dying.

Through a somnolent morning they rode up the Yellowstone valley seeing nothing. No one chased them. Massed trees usually kept them from being seen from the south bank, and on the rare occasions when no cover existed, they studied the far bank carefully before venturing out. Occasional trains rattled by across the river.

At Horse Creek, an intermittent tributary that now consisted only of occasional puddles, they turned northwest as planned, following a deepening coulee away from the great river. It would take them to the almost invisible divide separating the Musselshell drainage. Elwood rode up to a shoulder and studied the backtrail again, seeing nothing. The earth had baked into tile, and their hoofprints had grown fainter. It'd take an expert tracker to follow them now, especially with lively zephyrs whipping grit and dust into the faint prints.

Filomena slipped into silence as deep as that of the rest of them. She looked bedraggled. Dust had smeared her dress. Her hair hung in damp tendrils. Dark sweatmarks stained her bodice and armpits. Black circles marred the flesh under her soft eyes. Her gaze settled on one and another, most often on Elwood, who felt its probing. He winced at it, knowing what she thought of him.

Late in the weary day, they climbed a long grade and topped the divide. Elwood paused there, taking advantage of the sweeping view in all directions, studying the open country clear back to Miles City, lost in heat haze to the east. Nothing was dogging them except their own consciences.

"We'll rest the horses," he said.

"Help me with Con," Dillingham said.

Con Luce slumped before Angus, his chin on his chest, oblivious to the world. The man was unconscious; whether simply from sleep, Elwood couldn't tell. He helped Dillingham ease Luce into the grass. The erstwhile mine superintendent was breathing shallowly and seemed hotter than ever. Elwood ached for a physician. If only Toole could be here; Toole the doctor, not Toole the man who might be chasing them in order to hang them.

Filomena watched while Elwood felt Luce's forehead for heat and studied the hardness of the man's distended belly, which now pressed against his belt. Elwood loosened the belt.

"He needs to be cooled," she said. "The fever'll take him, if nothing else." Without asking, she pulled Elwood's canteen from his saddle and splashed water over Luce's blue cambric shirt, spreading it evenly until a dark patch of moist shirt clung to Luce. Then, without Ferrero's leave, she plucked a red bandanna from his pocket. He turned, startled, but said nothing. She soaked it in the cool water and anchored the compress over Constantine Luce's forehead. Time ticked by as she nursed the wounded man, applying fresh water until she'd used the whole of Elwood's canteen. Luce's breathing deepened and slowed. His eyes flickered open, revealing pools of pain and sorrow, studied Filomena, and closed again.

"Thank you," he whispered. "Kindness for a murderer."

"Don't say that," she replied. "Don't say it!"

Death had been driven away, at least for one tender moment.

The sun took remorse on the weary party and slid behind a long flat cloud in the west, and at once the prairie felt cooler. Astleheim found a spring up a slope and filled canteens. "Gyp," he said, "but not bad."

"Enough for the horses?"

"Yah."

Elwood made his decision. From where he stood on the divide, he could see the bend of the Musselshell River. A hundred yards away stood a thicket of cedar with a lot of dead branches. Firewood. "It's early, but we'll stay. Down there. We can get some tea into Con. He'll be a lot better in the morning. He's past the crisis now."

Elwood wasn't very sure of that. The others didn't look like they believed him. But Filomena nodded gravely. They unloaded horses and in ten minutes they had a camp at the cedar brake and a tiny smokeless fire flaring from tinder-dry cedar sticks.

"What's gyp water?" Filomena asked.

He'd not been aware she stood nearby. "Why, alkaline water. It's drinkable, I guess. If it's too alkaline it becomes— ah, a cathartic."

She smiled wryly. "I'll try some."

"We can mix it. We've good water in canteens still. You go wash if you want."

"I will," she said, but she didn't move. She stood beside him, her velvety gaze raking him with feathers. "I hope Con Luce doesn't die," she said.

He realized suddenly that she'd been nursing the man ever

since they'd stopped. Soaking his shirt, cooling him down, lowering his fever. "I didn't thank you," he responded.

"I'm a Drogovich, and I owe it."

"You don't owe anything. We owe you; we've taken away your liberty. And anyway, you're not your father. You're two different people, you and your father. You're you—as much a victim as any of us . . . before we became victimizers."

"This wouldn't have happened but for him."

"It was our choice. We're grown men."

"I'm not so sure grown men control their destiny that much. Or women. I'm not even sure my papa is doing what he wants. None of you wanted to be train robbers."

She was excusing him. It affected him deeply. "That's partly true. I got very dashing about it. I stood in my rooms twirling a revolver like real bandits."

"I don't suppose they twirl revolvers. They're more businesslike than you."

She had him there, he thought.

They stood side by side and watched Dillingham make tea, pour a cup, add sugar, and then feed it sip by sip to Con Luce with great tenderness. And all the while they watched, Elwood Attabury III was coming to a decision.

"Filomena," he said softly. She eyed him quietly. "Take your mare and go. Go back. Take the valuables—the stuff we took from passengers. That was just done to conceal us, but it burns in our hands. We hate what's in those sacks. It didn't conceal us at all. If you must, tell them who we are. The others'll understand. We'll scatter."

"No," Filomena said. "I'm staying."

Manny Claghorne's livery barn horse refused to budge. He kicked it and cussed it, but it rooted itself to the hard clay.

"Toole, it won't go."

Santiago surveyed the sullen animal, which stood with its legs locked and its ears flattened back. He understood the horse better than he understood Claghorne. For hours the railroad dick had sawed at the reins, reeled and wobbled in

the saddle, booted the poor animal, babbled periodically between long dreamy silences induced by the Dover's Powder.

"You're torturing it, Claghorne. Don't yank its head
around—that hurts its mouth. Leave some slack in your
reins—don't draw them up tight. When you tug on the reins,
you're telling it to stop."

"That's what I'm telling it all right. Teach that nag not to
run away with me."

"Look, Claghorne. This isn't working. I want to do this
alone. And you're not a man to be riding a horse. Now, lad,
you'd better get off and walk. It'll help your legs when the
powder loses its effect."

"Yeah," said Claghorne. He avalanched off again, so fast
that Toole thought he'd end in a heap. The nag lowered its
head and locked its legs. "I'm walkin' on pillows," he said.
"This stuff. You gonna make me an addict."

"I'm trying hard not to."

"I want some more."

"You'll get even less. You're going to hurt before I help."
He eyed the armed railroad man uneasily, not knowing what
sort of explosive combination Dover's Powder and a man
with a revolver might produce. He was in a fine fix, twenty
miles from Miles City with a man who couldn't ride and who
was half crazy on the anodyne. "I don't know what to do
with you. We can't go on."

"You going alone? What are you, some kinda hero? You
against all them train robbers? A gloryhound, that's what."

Toole sighed. "No, not alone against all those robbers.
But I'm going to shadow them. And steal their horses if I
can. They won't take that gold—or themselves—anywhere
without horses. That's a one-man job, Claghorne. It's a long
walk back, but that's the way it is. You lead that horse and
walk. I'll leave a dose with you—but don't take it until you
can't stand walking, understand?"

"Toole, did I ever tell you about the train that ate the
tallowpot?"

"The what?"

"The fireman. They was highballing along, and he was

shoveling coal. You know how much they shovel? A ton every twenty minutes, right into the box. Anyway, they hit a cow, bam! That old tallowpot, he sails right into the firebox and made steam.'' He grinned crazily. ''Well, that's me on this train. How'm I supposed to walk back to Miles? I got corns, and new ankletops not broke in yet.''

''All right,'' Toole said. He wished he'd never given the man the anodyne. ''I'm going to lead your horse.'' He slid off his thoroughbred and studied the livery barn bridle on Manny's beast. It was a sturdy affair with a noseband and throat latch. He unbuckled the bit from the headstall. Then he unbuckled the two reins from the bit and tied the ends together, making a lead line which he buckled to the ring under the nag's jaw. He slid the bit into Claghorne's saddle kit.

''All right. Get on. I've made a halter and I'm going to lead you. Just sit. Don't weary the horse in any way.''

''You gonna lead me? It ain't gonna take off?''

Toole shook his head. Claghorne mounted.

''I saw a runaway horse trolley once on Cicero Avenue. It jumped the rails and crashed into an organ grinder with a monkey. Killed the monkey and the accordion. I never trusted nags since. Now I got my hands loose, I'll hold my piece to its head. It starts running, I blow its brains out.''

''You better let me have your weapon. You're on a narcotic that . . . affects the mind.''

''Nothin' doing.''

''Well, my lad, don't you touch it,'' Toole said.

Claghorne clambered onto the sidestepping nag. ''Ow, I want more of that stuff.''

''No!'' Toole yelled.

He started again, yanking the reluctant horse along behind him, his mood growing more foul by the minute. But the livery nag settled into a walk and didn't need tugging.

He made good time for several hours, following rain-dimpled but clear tracks westward, leading the railroad dick along like a prisoner of war. The man settled into a reverie, eyeing the universe from under his cocked derby, at least until noon.

"I hurt," he announced.

"No!" Toole yelled, astonishing himself by his own vehemence.

"My legs, they'll die on me."

"You wouldn't go back."

"Toole, could we stop?"

"No. I'm hunting down railroad robbers. You do what you want."

"Could you get me across the river? I'll flag a train."

"You can answer that yourself."

"How much do you get paid?"

"Not enough."

"Let's flag a train. I'll make it worthwhile."

Toole sighed and ignored him. They rode on quietly, but that lasted only a few minutes.

"Toole. I'm gonna shoot this horse."

Santiago turned. Claghorne had extracted a wicked-looking revolver and was pressing the barrel into the back of the horse's head behind the ears.

"No!" he cried.

"Pills," Claghorne said.

Toole halted and slid off. Claghorne drugged would be easier to handle than Claghorne in pain. "All right. You're taking them at your own risk. They capture a man and eat him."

"Gimme the whole box. I'll shoot the horse."

Toole dug in his kit and found the box. He lifted the flap, poured half of the Dover's Powder capsules loose into the saddlebag, and shut the box again. God only knew who'd be injured and desperate when he caught up with the train robbers. He handed the pasteboard box to Claghorne, who instantly extracted two capsules and wolfed them down.

"You should save them for real trouble. What if you're shot?"

Claghorne grinned and slid the little box into the vest pocket of his pinstriped coat, somewhere near the nest of his shoulder-holstered revolver. "Yeah," he said. "Yeah. Let's get this outfit moving."

It didn't take long. In a couple of minutes Claghorne was grinning like an idiot. Toole didn't mind. He rode west again, leading the livery nag while Claghorne hummed "Rock of Ages," then "Amazing Grace," and then "A Mighty Fortress is Our God."

Later in the afternoon he lost the dimpled tracks. That had happened periodically, and he pushed ahead expecting to pick them up again. But after a mile or so he grew concerned and zigzagged from the river to the bluffs, hoping to cut sign. He found nothing.

"You're going every way but up," Claghorne said.

"I'm glad you're observant, Claghorne."

He could go farther upriver or he could retreat to the last sighting. He retreated, riding east, feeling the folly of this whole business upon him. Claghorne had ceased his humming, which secretly pleased Toole. He worked back to the place where Horse Creek debouched from the bluffs, and found faint tracks leading up the dry creekbed.

They'd left the Yellowstone here and were plunging into unsettled country. Well, he'd follow. And he'd also leave a message just in case a posse was following. With his camp hatchet he blazed two cottonwoods near the turnoff and then led Claghorne into a shallow coulee reaching northwest, finding shadowy sign here and there. The horse sign had crusted brown, but when he stopped and kicked some of it apart, he found bright green. He knew the train robbers—this Attabury and Con—were gaining ground and might continue to gain as long as he had to tug his drugged railway dick along. But he had little choice. They had their problems too: a gravely injured man, for one. And a hostage, for another.

He resolved to watch closer. If the one called Con died, they'd likely try to hide the body. If Drogovich's girl escaped—a real possibility from what he'd garnered about her—he'd need to keep a sharp eye out for sign. Strips of cloth, hoofprints going off somewhere, anything.

He was dragging deadweight, but so were they. He'd catch up if he kept his horses rested.

"Claghorne," he said. "We'll rest the nags up at the willows."

Manny Claghorne grinned back and clung to the saddle horn. "I can't get off," he said.

Chapter 15

Graff Biddle got the picture from the vestibule of the coach even before Fifty-six wheezed to an unscheduled stop at Bighorn. The burg sported little more than a saloon hostelry and a cluster of shacks. Some patient horses were anchored to the hitchrail. A few gents rather like himself lounged around, eyeing the westbound train curiously.

Biddle leapt down to the cinder roadbed before the screeching of the brakes had ceased, dragging his portmanteau with him. Behind him a brakeman waved and the Baldwin belched steam from its hips and chuffed forward toward the trestle over the Big Horn River. A man lounged there. One of Drogovich's crew. Dumb, all of them. Biddle chortled to himself. Amateurs. Any bunch of professional train robbers would sail past this little trap. It pleased him to possess a knowledge of the ways of the world.

He hefted his pigskin bag and closed the grassy gap between himself and the joint, furtively surveying the gents who were furtively surveying him. The place would be full-up, but he had his methods. They would not mistake him for a drummer even though he wore a green sharkskin suit with chalky pinstripes and a purple polka-dot cravat with a gold-plated watch fob dangling over his waistcoat. Railroad dicks just didn't look like drummers. It had something to do with the eyes. He'd always theorized that drummers had greedy eyes and dicks had mean eyes. His own were ice-brown. That was a description he'd invented. He'd never seen brown ice.

Graff Biddle's loyalties lay in two directions: toward him-

142

self and the Northern Pacific. He might or might not get along with lawmen, but regarded them mostly as nuisances. If he were to report everything he did to the law, and every felony and misdemeanor on two feet, he'd never help the N.P. none. Most of the bindlestiffs he'd tossed off boxcars were walking misdemeanors; but he'd derailed a few felonies too.

The proprietor of this dump would be pouring foam behind the bar. They all did. So he bulled through an open door into a dark coolness. The man was there, all right, his hair divided in the center and pomaded down with Vapo-Cresolene.

"Gimme a room," he said.

"We're full-up, buster."

"Gimme a room anyway," Biddle said, this time displaying his nickel-plated N.P. Inspector badge in its pigskin folder.

"That don't change us being full-up."

"Oh, it does. This here sits on deeded N.P. land. You want to give me a room?" Actually, Biddle had no idea whether the dump rested on deeded land. It never mattered. The terror of a land-title war with the railroad's shysters was enough. Always enough.

The man sighed. "I'll see what I can do."

"Tell Drogovich to let loose a room."

The man eyed Biddle warily. "You here because of that stuff too?"

"That's me."

From the shadowed rear of the saloon rose a quiet voice: "You."

Biddle turned and discovered a hulking presence in a dark corner, a man who looked like a well-dressed mortician.

"I am Drogovich."

Biddle felt the tables turning. What was it about the man? He found himself steering around battered tables and chairs toward the authority emanating from the corner.

"Mr. Drogovich," Biddle said, extending a meaty hand. The gold king did not shake it. Biddle extracted his hand from the no-man's-land between them and restored it to his side self-consciously.

"Why are you here?"

The question annoyed Biddle. "For the same reason you're here," he replied.

"The matter is taken care of."

"Ah, no. I have my duties. One of them is to interview you."

"The matter is taken care of."

"The N.P. has sent me to investigate and—"

"The robbers are known."

"Then you'll tell me who they are."

"Did Toole send you?"

"The sheriff? We talked briefly."

"He would have told you to find out about his woman. She's here. Is Toole following?"

"He's found a trail. He's—"

"A trail. It'll lead here. Has he a posse?"

"Naw. Just Manny Claghorne, far as I know."

"Claghorne?"

"The other inspector."

"Two railroad dicks." He pondered that. "He was told not to come here. So he sent you. It'll go hard on him. It'll go hard on you. When's the next through train? You'll want to be on it."

Drogovich was dismissing him. Dismissing the Northern Pacific Railroad. Dismissing the law. Biddle poked his derby back with his forefinger and grinned. "Some trap you got," he said. "You couldn't catch Jesse James's grandmother."

"I am Drogovich."

"Drogovich, listen to a railroad dick. How many sidings are there between here and Miles, eh?"

Drogovich neither replied nor shifted his penetrating gaze.

"There's four." Biddle said no more, and enjoyed the spectacle of the gold king pretending to know everything. "How many freights come on through since the robbery?"

Drogovich remained silent.

"Three westbound, two eastbound. How many come on

through at night? How many sat on one of them four sidings?
Ya don't know, do ya? Them bandits, they're probably west
ah here. Unless you stopped all them freights and searched
every boxcar. Ya didn't. Ya watched the ferries and ya had a
man at the trestle lookin' for foot traffic. One thing any train
robber's good at is jumping freights. Even with horses sometimes. If a brakeman catches them, too bad for the brakeman.
Drogovich, you got a train robbery, you gotta get expert
advice.''

Drogovich's sole response was a long expulsion of breath.
Biddle felt exultant. He'd bested a gold baron; he'd shoved
the old bull moose, and the old bull moose backed up.

''You don't even know them bandits are goin' west,'' he
added. ''You cooperate with the Northern Pacific Railroad
and we'll get somewhere.''

''Drogovich owns the Northern Pacific.''

''One percent.'' That was a guess. Biddle knew who really
owned the N.P. But it was a good guess. Drogovich's pupils
dilated slightly.

''What is your name?''

''Graff Biddle.''

''You earn forty-seven fifty a month—and extras.''

It was Biddle's turn to be surprised. Not only about the
wage, but about the extras. A railroad dick collected bo-
nuses. He cleaned out tinhorn gamblers before tossing them
out of Pullman Palace cars. He grabbed the pokes of the
bindlestiffs he ejected. Some dicks padded their purses with
the offerings of swindlers, candy butchers, monte players,
and tarts who wanted to stay aboard a Pullman.

''Drogovich'll hire you for fifty.''

''Fifty! I got a good job with the N.P.''

''Drogovich knows.''

''What's this Drogovich stuff? Can't you say I?''

Drogovich smiled and ignored him. ''Biddle, what's the
price of your soul?''

''I'm not for sale. I like the railroad.''

''Your soul. Your price. What worldly thing do you want?''

''Look, Drogovich. Sometimes I pocket a few bucks. I let

some swindler stay aboard for a double eagle. I do that. But I don't do the heavy stuff. The N.P. hires me, the N.P.'s got me. You can't hire me. You ain't gonna butcher some train robbers and throw them into the river with me keeping quiet. You ain't goin' to hurt some lawman's woman without my telling the world. I ain't special, but I got a line I don't cross. I don't even like the boodle I get for ignoring the rules. I do it but I don't like it when I do. Naw, Drogovich. I'm an inspector and a good one. Everything that happens here I'll tell the N.P.''

Drogovich smiled. ''An honorable man. Better than Drogovich. They're all better than Drogovich. Elwood Attabury, a gentleman and a builder. Con Luce, another gentleman and a leader. Dr. Toole, an idealist. His woman Mimi, a courageous one. And Inspector Graff Biddle—dirty on the edges but clean inside. It's a pity. You looked so buyable. Drogovich is poor company among ones so honorable. But he has a soul too.''

Graff Biddle studied the gold baron, wondering if the man was unbalanced. It didn't matter. ''Drogovich—you lost 'em here. They either rode through on a freight or they rode somewhere else. These here names, Attabury and Luce. You knew them before the robbery, right?''

Drogovich didn't reply. The man had a maddening way of not responding to questions.

''This Luce—he's the Con that Toole treated. Toole, he read your wires off the telegrapher's spindle and you read his. You each had a piece of the answer. Only you know more'n him. These here polite bandits Toole told me about, they really was after your gold. Maybe it was their gold. They weren't real bandits, Toole says. More like amateurs. Maybe businessmen. Makes me wonder who to pinch. Maybe you're all tied up in it.''

''It was Fate,'' Drogovich said. He lifted a hand, and a man mysteriously appeared from the vicinity of the bar. ''My assistant, Arnold Carp,'' Drogovich said.

Biddle beheld a gaunt man whose face was unacquainted with the sun. Biddle knew the type. He'd studied phrenology and knew a long skull with a prominent bulge over the ears when he saw one.

Carp cleared his throat and mumbled.

"Mr. Carp will show you to your room," Drogovich said.

"You gonna let me have a room, Drogovich?"

"Certainly."

"Life's fulla surprises."

Carp beckoned, so Biddle hoisted his portmanteau and followed through a rear door of the hostelry and toward the barn, which seemed odd to the railroad dick.

Constantine Luce died about the time they reached the Musselshell River. Elwood was holding him that afternoon, keeping the comatose man upright in the saddle before him. The change was so subtle that at first Elwood wasn't sure. But then he halted the overburdened horse and eased Constantine to the ground. They all gathered around the inert form, finding no pulse or breath, and a new stillness that announced the passage from mortal life. Elwood grieved but there was nothing to say. Luce himself had said that what was done was done; there was only the future to consider.

No one spoke.

"We'll take him with us," he said.

A decent burial for the mine superintendent would be a problem. They had no shovel. They needed to conceal the body because Luce would be recognized by Drogovich or others; the discovery of the body would expose them all.

They pulled panniers off a packsaddle and distributed the load, and then anchored Con Luce over it, an indignity to the dead but unavoidable. Then they rode quietly into the evening, keeping their thoughts to themselves. The mood of the little party had darkened.

They followed the cottonwood-lined Musselshell River westward through a wilderness. There were no settlements there, although a few ranchers had established themselves in the grassy infinities of the open range.

The death had affected Filomena as much as anyone else, and she rode solemnly through the deepening light. Elwood found himself lonely and thought the others were lonely too. Death did that. In its terrible presence mortals found themselves alone, and filled with the dread of knowing. They were all going to come to that great divide.

Filomena adroitly spurred her horse forward to ride abreast of Elwood, seeming to want the silent company even though she said nothing. He too wanted the company, even of the acid-tongued young woman. Something odd had happened: she really didn't seem to mind the abduction, seemed to count it an adventure even though her barbed comments remained exactly as before.

"I'm looking for a place to bury him," he said. "A cutback we can cave in over him. Something like that. He deserves that."

She said nothing. He'd expected her to retort that train robbers didn't deserve a good burial.

"Con had the gifts I lack," he said. "He turned my gold strike into a mine. I'm a good geologist. I can read surfaces and guess what's under them. But it took Con Luce to organize it all; raise capital, order supplies, hire miners, and all the rest. He did it brilliantly."

"That's what attracted my father."

A wave of bitterness seeped through Elwood. "There are builders, and there are robbers and politicians preying on the achievements of others," he said.

She laughed mercilessly—and then suddenly stopped. "I'm sorry," she said. "I'm sorry."

"I am too." He sighed. "I'll have to let Melanie know. His widow. He had two daughters and a son."

"Elwood—really, my daddy's to blame."

He peered at her amazed. "I can't parcel blame," he said at last. "We're all responsible for our own conduct. I'm more to blame than your father. Con Luce wasn't to blame: I talked him into this. He didn't want to. He did it for me against his deepest instincts. They all joined in against their deepest instincts."

"Yes, but something terrible had happened to them all,"

she said. "My father came upon you like one of the horse-
men of the Apocalypse bringing darkness to you."

She was excusing them. He turned to her, finding her solemn and her gaze upon him. He discovered a Filomena he'd
scarcely imagined before; not the spoiled cruel beauty of
legend, but a serious young woman without blind loyalties.

"Miss—Miss Drogovich," he stammered. "I'm doomed.
Maybe the words of a doomed man are more sincere because
of that very fact. But I wish I might have known you under
other circumstances. You're—lovely."

"And you're a train robber." She mocked him again.

He rode ahead silently, the specter of prison upon him
once more. He cursed himself for playing the fool.

They passed through a dense cottonwood forest and out
upon a bankside park rank with tall grasses now that no
buffalo grazed it down. His geologist's eye noted the wind-
sculptured sandstone outcrops in the bluffs and the dark jackpine that dotted the upper reaches of the rugged hills.

"What's that?" she asked.

His gaze followed the vector of her pointed finger. She
was pointing at some scaffolding in young cottonwoods. He
knew at once it was an Indian burial place. He'd read about
them but never seen one. He steered his horse off the trail
and toward the south bluffs toward the place. She followed.

Before them stood an ancient cemetery of a tribe unknown. Most of the platforms were wedged into trees, cross-
pieces lashed into forked limbs with rawhide, well above eye
level. But a few had been built upon four posts planted in the
earth. One of the platforms had caved in, spilling its weathered contents: an ancient buffalo robe, dessicated almost to
dust; and within it, human skeletal remains. A bleached skull,
darker ribs. Some obscure bundles littered the place, along
with a bow bleached gray by the relentless sun.

"They buried their people on platforms. They didn't have
metal shovels," he said. "I don't know the tribe. Crow,
Sioux, Blackfoot probably."

"Well?" she said.

It took him a moment to grasp the direction of her thought.

She always seemed ahead of him. "But—it's a heathen place," he said slowly. "It's not—a Christian place."

Her face screwed up into scorn and then returned to placidity. "It's a haven for Mr. Luce. No one'll ever find him here. What more could you ask?"

She was right.

The others drew up and studied the ancient burial place solemnly. Elwood rode from scaffold to scaffold, studying the silent mounds on them. Some of the Indians had been wrapped and bound in white men's blankets, now faded or weathered to tatters, others in buffalo robes that had turned light and brittle. Some scaffolds bore two bodies, perhaps a husband and wife or parent and child. Some had collapsed, spilling desiccated remains. Animals had scattered bones and debris. Back toward the bluff, he found a tree scaffold that had been built wide for two, but contained only one long bundle. Nearby on the ground lay an ancient green blanket that the elements had blown from somewhere. It would do. Constantine Luce would lie with a strange people—and be safe forever. At least if the Drogovich woman didn't tattle.

"Here," he said. The others, who had drifted behind him, stopped. They needed no instruction. Tenderly they lifted Constantine Luce off the packhorse and straightened his resisting body. It no longer would lie flat, but with patience Astleheim worked Luce's limbs out. Chico recovered the ancient blanket which had faded to some indeterminate pastel shade.

They wrapped the mortal coil of Constantine Luce in it and tied it with twine from their kit and settled it on the scaffold beside the other unknown person. Two warriors, thought Elwood. Then they stood below. The body had vanished into the ancient silence of an Indian burial ground.

"Aren't you going to say something?" Filomena asked.

It piqued him. "I'll ask you to say something, Miss Drogovich."

They all waited, and he saw curiosity and dread in their faces. The last of the day's sun caught in her brass hair. She didn't know what to say, and he saw she was puzzling out words.

"He was a good husband and father and mine manager and friend. He was a train robber, murderer, and kidnapper of women. What else should I say?"

No one answered.

"You all loved him. And because you did, I do too. And maybe God does too."

She said that to Elwood, her gaze locked in his. It seemed less a burial than a birth.

Chapter 16

Much to Santiago's surprise, Manny Claghorne turned himself into a good rider in the space of two days. To be sure, the Dover's Powder helped Claghorne sit easily in the saddle and absorb the movement of the horse under him. But Claghorne was also working at it. Periodically he dismounted and walked, leading his horse and exercising his aching legs. In that small space of time, Santiago had come to respect and even enjoy the determined railroad dick.

"Are we gainin'?" Claghorne asked.

"A little. At least we have a trail—if it doesn't rain the way it did."

"You think that gunshot one's gonna cash in?"

Toole nodded. "He might make it in a bed—with total rest and medical attention."

"How do you figger this Drogovich?"

Toole sighed. He'd been trying to figure Drogovich for three days, worried sick about Mimi, who was caught in his thoughts hour after hour. A hostage. One who could be easily hurt. Hurt in a way that'd hurt Santiago forever. Stay away or she'll be hurt, Drogovich had said to him. But Santiago knew he wouldn't stay away: somehow, some way, he'd slip through the gold baron's private army and arrest the man for kidnapping.

"He frightens me," Toole said.

Manny looked as if he'd just heard a confession. "I never heard no sheriff say that," he said. "You're an honest one, Toole. It must be the Irish."

"More the doctor. I deal with calamity. Most of the time I can do nothing."

"Scairt. They'll hold it against you at elections."

Santiago smiled. They hadn't held it against him for three elections.

"Well, that Drogovich. He's got ol' Biddle after him now. The N.P., it don't take no guff."

Santiago didn't reply. He believed the other N.P. dick wouldn't even slow Drogovich down. The gold king was going to wage his private war no matter who got hurt. "Pray for Mrs. Toole," he said.

Manny glanced at him sharply. Toole knew he didn't talk like sheriffs, especially Western sheriffs.

They topped a low divide, found where the bandits had camped at an alkaline spring, and followed the trail toward the distant valley of the Musselshell. With each hour, they were pulling farther away from Bighorn on the Yellowstone River, where Drogovich waited futilely to spring his trap. In a way, that was good. He wanted the bandits safe in his Miles City jail before Drogovich even knew of it.

"You got vittles?"

Santiago realized the man was starved. He'd brought little food and that had vanished long before. Toole could get along for days with almost nothing to eat if his mind was focused on a problem so much that he scarcely heard the cries of his own body. But the railroad dick would be starved.

"I'll have to hunt."

"How do you do it, Toole? For days I'm starving. But I keep my yap shut. Don't say nothin'. This here sheriff'll feed me. My stomach, it's pushin' on my backbone, Toole. I says to myself I'm as good as him, I can last as long as him, but me, I'm just a greengrocer's son from South Chicago. You got anything at all?"

"Tea. A little sugar for it."

"That sounds like steaks to me."

"We'll strike the Musselshell in an hour. There'll be game in there. And firewood." The sweep of his arm would remind Claghorne that there wasn't a stick in sight.

"I prefer sittin' in a Palace car sippin' bourbon and keepin' an eye on the monte dealer."

Toole's fondness for the detective grew. For two days Claghorne had starved and never complained! And even now, in the midst of his starvation, he kept his humor. They reached the river bottom without seeing any game. Toole really didn't want to fire his rifle anyway: the report could reach those ahead. But he brewed Earl Grey tea over a small campfire, dosed it liberally with sugar, and watched Claghorne suck it down like an Irishman at his ale.

"That's a start. Where's the potatoes, Toole?"

"In the ground, Manny. They're tiny in June but I'll collect some—maybe."

The detective grinned and clambered aboard his horse. He was improving each day—and taking less of the Dover's Powder. They rode through an arched afternoon, following the clear trail of broken grasses, occasional prints in the dust, and browning horse sign. Toole wasn't enough of a tracker to count horses, but he guessed ten or twelve. They burst into a grassy area, and beyond it a park loosely dotted with cottonwoods.

"What are them things?" Manny asked.

"We're in the presence of the dead, Manny. The plains people bury them on scaffolds."

"Damn savages."

"They give them to the sun, Manny. They're horrified that we put them in the earth."

"Heathen, that's what they are."

"My wife's neither savage nor heathen."

"Aw, Toole."

Santiago discovered tracks veering off to the burial grounds, and followed them. The bandits were sightseeing, perhaps. Maybe robbing scaffolds.

"I don't wanna go close to no Injun cemetery."

They sat their horses staring at the somber place. Claghorne kept his silence out of some innate respect. Here and there over several acres scaffolds hung like nests in trees, or rose on four posts from the grasslands along the river. The tracks led nowhere. Apparently the bandits had done their sightseeing and continued onward unhurried, not believing that they were being followed. Frowning, Toole turned back, some faint sensation tickling the back of his mind. He could put no name to it, so they continued onward through the deepening evening, adding a dozen more miles before the summer sun slid toward the far western horizon.

That's when the thing that had clawed at him the rest of the afternoon popped into his mind: he'd smelled, ever so subtly, the odor of putrefying flesh there in a place where the sun had long since desiccated all the Indian remains. *The one called Con.*

"Manny, we'll stop here to rest the horses. Picket your horse—and don't start a fire. I'm going to walk to that hilltop and have a look ahead with my glass. We're close now."

"I'm runnin' outa them powders."

"Then suffer, Claghorne."

Toole found malicious pleasure in it. He walked wearily toward a knob that rose above the south bluff. He'd scarcely slept since the night the bandits had come for help. The nights on the trail hadn't rested him: he'd pushed into dark each evening and forced Claghorne onto his tired horse long before dawn, trusting they'd pick up the tracks. The bandits were no better off; maybe worse.

Five hundred yards and one prairie rattler later, Toole eased himself onto the knob and extended his brass telescope. Patiently he glassed the country upriver, seeing nothing but bobbing cottonwoods and bouncing boulders. He was about to give up when he spotted movement, and finally gazed upon a tiny knot of ants, too small to number, caught by the setting sun. Two, maybe three miles ahead. Closer than he'd imagined.

"All right," he said aloud. He studied them a moment longer, fearful that the dying sun would blaze in his lens and alert them; collapsed his field glass and crabbed back off the knob. His mind ached with possibilities, but there was only one salient idea: he'd try to grab their horses immediately. That night.

He found Manny with his britches off and his rear end lowered into the river.

"If you laugh, I'll kill you, Toole."

Toole laughed. Manny didn't kill him.

"I saw them. Not far ahead."

"Yeah?" Manny came alert in a hurry.

"We're riding. I'm going for their horses tonight."

"I'm starved."

"Eat that," Toole said, pointing at cattails. "Eat the roots. It's Indian food."

"In South Chicago I could get beefsteak any time, day or night. Beefsteak and sauerkraut."

Toole yanked cattails out of the bankside muck and washed the knobby white roots. He tried one himself. He'd heard of it from Mimi but had never sampled the delicacy. The root stock was bland, hard to chew, but edible. She'd told him the Indians dried the root stock and ground it into a nourishing flour.

"I want real food," Manny said. "I wouldn't touch them weeds even if my mother told me. And anyways I just been pollutin' it."

Toole grinned. He fooled with Saint James, rubbing the thoroughbred's back and pretending not to see pantless Claghorne, who was yanking up cattails the way a dentist yanks molars.

He let Claghorne masticate for a while and then saddled the horses. "Come on now," he said.

"You got more of that powder?"

"Walk. It'll ease the pain in your legs."

"Toole, you're a sadist. Makin' me eat weeds. Makin' me ride again. I'm a railroad dick not Buffalo Bill."

Nonetheless, Claghorne huffed and groaned to his feet and winced his way to the horse.

"I told you not to come."

"One more word from you, Toole, and I'll—"

"Want to stay here? Most of this is going to be on foot anyway. I can't take my horse close. They'll all start whinnying. I'll walk the last two miles."

"You gonna make me walk?"

"Ride and walk."

"I'm no expert horse thief, Toole. I got a railroad badge."

"I'll go alone. It's better that way."

"Don't leave me alone. You'll never find me again. Whadda I do if you get hurt?"

"Ride south to the rails."

"South, south. All I know is South Chicago."

"Manny, I'll find you. Just don't shoot me when I come in. With any luck I'll have a lot of horses."

"All alone I'm going ta be? What if something attacks me?"

Manny Claghorne looked genuinely frightened. But Santiago didn't want to take him along. "Just don't shoot. They can hear it."

"Toole, don't leave me."

But Santiago clambered wearily aboard his stallion and steered it upriver into the thickening dusk.

Ingmar Drogovich idly spread the cards before him in the gloom of the Bighorn saloon. He used playing cards to think. Something about the cards helped him to analyze situations and deal with them. He never sought advice; had never asked for the opinion of another mortal. But the cards helped him. He'd always reserved the spade suit for himself; he was the king of spades. Filomena the queen; Carp was the ten, and the rest were the small numbers. He didn't employ the aces. That was to keep himself humble; to remind himself that in this world lurked better men than himself.

He'd designated Elwood Attabury and his minions the diamond suit. It amused him to make Elwood the jack. Toole was king of hearts; the queen, the red queen, he held out in the tack room of the barn along with a low club, the railroad dick. He made the two Northern Pacific inspectors the nine and ten of clubs.

He laid out the diamonds, and added the queen of spades to that pile. He dropped the queen of hearts and nine of clubs in his spade pile. He set the king of hearts aside, not knowing how many other hearts—a posse perhaps—to add to that pile. Lack of information annoyed him. Bighorn had no station and no telegrapher, so he was temporarily cut off from news. Which was one thing he would remedy at once.

Simply by staring at that jack of diamonds, he realized he could discount Biddle's notion that the train robbers had jumped a freight train and escaped the trap here. Drogovich knew Elwood Attabury. The man had been the object of intense study. Drogovich knew that the geologist and engineer had too many scruples to do anything but flee pell-mell after the robbery. No. He and his gang didn't jump a freight and slide through Bighorn; they fled somewhere, not ever wanting to see a railroad again.

He paused amiably. Just by laying that jack of diamonds out on the battered table he'd come to some understanding. Biddle had worried him a little at first with his chapter-and-verse knowledge of the criminal brain. But Biddle didn't know Attabury. It was an odd thing Elwood Attabury had done. If the man had been a king rather than a jack, he'd have tried to wrest his mine back instead of going for a mere two hundred thousand in bullion—a small sum compared to the riches that lay embedded in the veins of the Fate. But he had a jack mind, and no doubt wanted merely a start on a new life. He'd kissed off the Fate.

But even if that nine of clubs now enjoying the amenities of the tack room had been wrong about what Attabury's gang might do, he did raise another point; one that nagged at Drogovich. That jack of diamonds was smart enough to see the trap beforehand and avoid it. Where, oh where, had the knave gone? What sense was there in staying here, ready to spring the jaws, if Attabury was heading somewhere else— with the king of hearts on his trail?

Drogovich extracted a gold Waltham pocket watch from his waistcoat and examined it closely as it ticked life away. It read nine-fifteen. Almost three days since the robbery a hundred miles to the east. Fleeing bandits would have come through Bighorn in that time, making forty or even fifty miles a day by driving their horses to their limit. The jaws of the trap remained open, but no prey entered. By dawn it'd be clear that Attabury had not come this way. A grudging admiration rose in Drogovich for the jack of diamonds.

He'd want his special in the morning. The boxcar, coach, and caboose still stood on the siding west of Bighorn, but the engine had long since steamed off after running low on coal. To move his cars in either direction his men would have to flag down a through train and have his cars coupled to it. He frowned, feeling trapped—and maybe outsmarted by that jack of diamonds.

He pondered the two queens, half amused. Filomena was in the hands of Attabury, where she'd come to absolutely no harm even if Attabury found himself being chased by posses, Toole, detectives, or Drogovich's own men. It was beyond the gentlemanly jack of diamonds to harm her. He could just as well have left her behind for all the good the hostage would do him. But that wasn't true of the queen of hearts. Toole loved his woman, and she loved him, and for almost three days Drogovich's men had occupied Bighorn without being molested or pursued by the sheriff. It was a good point: if you are going to take a hostage, you must be prepared to do what you threaten to do. Drogovich grimaced. Toole didn't know it, but he'd never see his savage wife again.

Drogovich sighed. He had no confessor. But several times in his life he'd unburdened himself upon a human scapegoat. It was a weakness he couldn't help. He wished he could be as devoid of conscience as those pirates Jay Gould or Daniel Drew in New York. But he'd never managed. If the world ever defeated him, it'd be because of that; because he required an occasional scapegoat to unburden his spirit and bring himself into some sort of peace. They all lived, of course: one could not cut the throat of a scapegoat. She would live—in a wilderness of his devising.

He turned his gaze at last to the other little pile: the king of hearts and ten of clubs, and maybe some other hearts if Toole had trackers and possemen with him. Toole had done the right thing—the lawman's thing—following the trail. Toole could catch up with the gentleman bandits and swiftly disarm them and recover the booty. He'd bring them back to Miles City for trial. There'd be lawyers. Reporters. Spectators. Probably an unbuyable judge. And publicity of a kind that Drogovich wished to avoid at all costs. It'd be Elwood's defense to show that the Fate had been stolen; that he'd been the victim of crooked judges and officials; that Drogovich was the spider in the center of that web. And Attabury would have little trouble proving it.

The thought triggered the decision. Once again, laying out playing cards had helped him see his way. He'd been debating taking his men back to Helena and pouncing quietly on Attabury there after the uproar died away. But he couldn't do that: not when a trial in Miles City would expose things he'd rather not see public. He knew what to do. He'd go to Miles City. With any luck he'd get there ahead of Toole.

That Toole. Drogovich knew intuitively that the king of hearts would catch the jack of diamonds and all the jack's men. That Toole. An annoyance built up in Drogovich as it always did when he faced a competent opponent. But Toole, like himself, was vulnerable: Drogovich could play the queen of hearts.

"Carp," he said softly, knowing the low voice would be heard by the man at the bar.

Arnold Carp came at once, carrying his glass of what purported to be Crab Orchard whiskey but wasn't.

The sallow man stood before his master, a question in his face.

"We'll couple our cars to the eastbound freight that comes through here before dawn and go back to Miles. Send a rider out to the siding now to alert the brakeman we hired—if he's still there. If not, get some of our men out there to flag the freight."

"You think they got through?"

"I don't think anything. When the freight gets here with our cars on the end, put the Toole woman and railroad dick in our caboose and don't let them out. In Miles, keep them out of sight."

"Anything else?"

"When we get to Miles, find out which way Toole went and with who. He'll be bringing in Attabury. You'll make sure they never get into Miles."

"If you say so," Carp said.

Chapter 17

Mimi surveyed the man who had been pushed into the tack room of the barn. Just enough light of the dying day filtered through the cracks to reveal a blocky fellow in a gaudy green suit, cravat, and derby. She peered at him fearfully: he had the look about him of one of Drogovich's men.

He'd been planted there to engage her in talk, to learn what he could about Santo. Resolutely she said nothing and let the scorn in her dark face do her talking for her. The guard would be listening too; probably had his ear to the door. She surveyed this one, looking for something else; the raptor's look of a man with a helpless woman. He could do what he would: no one would hear her screams—or care.

She eyed the implements and harness about her, seeking a weapon. And found several: a rasp, a nippers, several horseshoes, some hames, a hoof-paring knife. Maybe she'd fight. They'd stop her, of course. Outside they listened. With the first noise of a scuffle they'd swing open the door and stop her from defending herself.

The man settled himself opposite her, his back to the planks of the inner wall. He studied her momentarily and then eyed the harness and tools, registering each item with care.

"Mrs. Toole, I believe."

The man had a reedy voice and an Eastern inflection. He'd come from some city. She decided not to respond.

He waited and then said, "I don't blame youse. Fine fix you're in. Here. Can you still see this?"

He withdrew something wallet-sized from the breast pocket of his suit and handed it to her. Within was a shining metal badge of some sort. It confused her. She knew intuitively he was no lawman. It'd grown too dark for her to read.

"It says, Inspector Nine, Northern Pacific Railroad Company. I'm a railroad dick. Graff Biddle's the name. We'll be enjoying this joint together—until Drogovich lets us loose."

She wanted to tell him that Drogovich wasn't going to let her loose, but she held her silence.

"Don't wanna say nothing, eh? I don't blame ya. Ya figure I'm his man too. Ya got a good husband there in Miles and he's plenty worried. Asked me to look after ya, and let me tell ya, that look in his eyes when he said it—he's a carin' man. Me and Claghorne, we took the westbound outa Bismarck, where we're based, to have us a lookee into this robbery. He met us and says that Drogovich, he's taken you as hostage and he's headin' here to try to spring a trap. He said he's got him a trail to foller, and he's got him a tracker he knows over to the saloon. So I get back on and come here, and Drogovich don't like me meddling, don't want the N.P. in on this, and I tell him the N.P.'s in it whether he wants it or not. He tries the old palm grease, and I tell him I can't be bought—and here I am."

It sounded plausible. Something was released in her. She sensed she wouldn't be assaulted. But she didn't trust him.

She stood and walked to the door, peered out of a crack, looked for her guard in the velvety lavender dusk. She saw him sitting on a stump yards away—out of earshot if they whispered. Distrusting, she peered through other cracks, seeing only the dusk. But she couldn't see through the cracks into the interior of the barn, which was wrapped in gloom. Someone might be there.

"You don't trust me," he said. "But anything you can tell me about Drogovich—that'll help me. What's he said to you?"

"I'll think about this," she whispered. She sat in companionable silence for several minutes, wanting to talk to him, aware that he had treated her respectfully. At last she decided to take the risk.

"What do you know about the Bible?" she asked.

"Huh? The what? Nothing much, but I tip my hat when we pass."

It made her laugh in spite of herself. "I can't get into any more trouble than I am, so I'll trust you," she said. "Listen closely because I'm going to whisper." She jabbed a finger at the inner wall. He nodded.

Slowly, breathing out her words so quietly that he strained to hear, she described her abduction from her home, the brief train ride, her swift imprisonment in the tack room, and then her strange interview with Drogovich shortly before.

"He fed me. He stared at me while I ate. His stare—I couldn't meet it. He seemed to know everything about me. At first—I wasn't very afraid. He looks—so civilized. You know. Well dressed. Manicured. Clean. Direct. But—Mr. Biddle—before he put me back here, I went through . . . one of the most awful experiences of my life. *Mon Dieu!* My future—it's worse than death!"

"Them rich men are like that. That's how they got it. Read everyone like open books. What's this Bible stuff, now?"

Hesitantly at first, fearing this man wouldn't believe her, she described Drogovich's confession: the stealing of the Fate from the one called Attabury, the bribery, the rough tactics, the bought judges.

"That's how Toole figures. He says this is no usual buncha robbers. Too polite. This here's the best stuff I've got so far."

That somehow relieved her. Santo had told her the same thing.

"You won't believe the rest," she whispered. "You'll just say I'm hysterical."

"I'm listenin'."

She told Biddle about what Drogovich had said about his parents; how he'd confessed to a conscience; how he'd seen the suffering of his father and mother in the faces of the miners and their wives his bullyboys had ruined; how he'd told her she was his confessor, and how frightening that news had been to her, sealing her doom. And then about the reading from Leviticus. "He called me his scapegoat!"

"And he's stuffin' you into the wilderness," he said.

"He told me where—the Sandwich Islands! I won't ever see Santo again!"

"Santo?"

"Santiago. I won't ever see him. I'll be—be sold. They like mixed-bloods there. That's what that man told me." Tears rose unbidden. She snuffled them back.

He didn't comfort her. He seemed absorbed with something. Night had lowered and now they could scarcely make out each other's presence. She could no longer see anything through the cracks except a star or two in the high, free heaven.

"Jaysas," he muttered. "You got this pegged?"

She didn't know what he alluded to, and waited.

"I'm a dead man."

She understood. Drogovich's secrets had spread to his ears.

She heard him clamber to his feet. She heard him poke and probe the walls and floor. He pushed on planks. Sometimes they squeaked. He fingered tack. He lifted the rasp and nippers. He lifted a horseshoe. It clanked against another when he set it down.

"We gotta bust out," he whispered. "You got any ideas?"

She didn't. "They'll hear," she whispered.

"Well, we don't get nowhere if we don't try."

She heard a systematic rasping. He was sawing through the planks at the rear of the tack room. The door swung open suddenly. Biddle had anticipated it and sprang, the murderous rasp in hand. For an instant his bulk darkened the doorway. But the guard had anticipated it too. She heard a heavy thud; a woof of expelled air; a gasp, and Biddle careened backward, tumbling to the floor over her legs.

The guard loomed in the doorway, blocking her view of the bright stars.

"Don't you move none," the guard said. "I'm listening. You try sawing your way out, and—" He didn't finish it. "Horsemeat," he said. "Horsemeat."

The door slammed shut. She felt grit settle on her. In the inkiness she felt Biddle struggle with himself, roll off her legs, and settle back into the opposite wall. He breathed hard and occasionally gasped. The man across from her hurt. She trusted him now.

"Are you bleeding?"

"Naw. But I sure got a headache. And a gutache."

"I wish I could help you."

"I don't suppose you got some booze?" He laughed suddenly.

She laughed too, crazily. They were both doomed, and the laughing drove back the night.

That's how the night bled away. Neither dozed. Sometimes they whispered. Mostly they sat silently, each alone; each nursing some vision of the future—or lack of it.

"Mrs. Toole," he said. "You're some lady. No matter what he does to you—you'll fight your way out."

"I wish I could believe it . . . But thank you, Mr. Biddle. Here you are, thinking of me at a moment when you're in trouble."

"You must be sicka hearin' confessions, but maybe you can stand another. Drogovich, he says, Biddle, you're dirty on the outside and clean inside. He's right. I wish I was clean all over. You're clean, Mrs. Toole. The Sandwich Islands— they ain't gonna make you unclean. You don't get dirty except as how it's your own free will doin' it. You follow me?"

"I do, Mr. Biddle. You're a good man in a hard business. You're a good man inside."

"Until death do us part," he said, laughing crazily again.

They lapsed into silence again for some interminable time. But then, while it was still dark, they were awakened by someone with a coal oil lantern, marched out of the tack room and through the darkened saloon and to the railroad tracks. After a while she watched her captors flag down an eastbound freight with lanterns, and she wondered where she would be taken. She felt like a steer en route to the stockyards.

* * *

As night thickened, Santiago rode up the valley of the Musselshell River through cottonwood timber, parks, and meadows. He didn't know how far ahead the robbers were: when he'd glassed them from the knob, they were still traveling into the setting sun. That complicated matters. He had a formidable task before him and wondered if he'd succeed— or whether he'd get into grave trouble. These bandits may have been polite, but they'd murdered the expressman and buffaloed a resisting passenger. He had to steal their horses— no easy task for a single man—and then negotiate with them. He'd made the right decision about Manny: the railroad dick would have been worse than useless around the horses.

After what he judged was a couple of miles of night riding, he steered his horse toward the bluff and ascended it cautiously. He was looking for a campfire ahead but saw none. It bothered him. Was his quarry slipping away through the night? He descended and rode upriver again, increasingly worried that his stallion would pick up the scent of other horses and bleat his greetings.

"Don't betray me, you blooming idjit," he said, running a hand up the silky flesh under the mane.

He paused frequently, straining to hear what lay ahead, but only the crickets greeted him. No moon illumined his way, but the sky was clear and open, and he found light enough if he was careful and stayed away from woods.

Thus he proceeded for another hour, occasionally ascending the bluffs on his left, seeing only an inky void and edging cautiously upriver again. Had they discovered him and Manny? Were they fleeing now—perhaps away from the river entirely?

He worked cautiously around a promontory that rose almost from the riverbank—and then it was too late. They had camped just beyond. Their horses neighed and whickered. His stallion snorted. They'd let their fire die in the warm night, so no flickering light had warned him. Dark figures rolled out of their blankets, reaching for weapons. A woman sat up. An excited horse pulled its picket pin up and sidled back into brush.

Toole did the only thing he could: he bluffed. "Don't move. Halt. Don't get hurt. This is the law!" he roared, reaching for his own holstered revolver.

To his surprise they did halt, but looked as if they might disobey at any moment.

"Who's Attabury?" Toole demanded.

A man unfolded from the ground, slowly. Toole couldn't make out his looks. "You found out after all," the man said. "There's nothing left."

That puzzled Toole a moment. "Drop your weapons, all of you. Then give me your names. Which of you is Con Luce? You'll need medical help."

"He's dead," Attabury said quietly.

The scaffold, Toole thought.

The sheepish train robbers stood. Those who had a weapon in hand carefully lowered it to the earth. Toole waited warily, fearful of trickery. But something told him they wouldn't resist. It was as if naming one of them had broken their will.

"Is that you, Miss Drogovich? Are you all right?"

"Don't ask asinine questions," she retorted.

Toole puzzled about that. His question hadn't been asinine at all. Satisfied that the sleepy men had surrendered, he pointed a finger at one. "Name?" he barked.

"Ferrero. Enrico Ferrero."

Toole's finger moved.

"Karl Astleheim."

"Chico."

"Angus Dillingham."

"You all worked at the Fate?"

Men nodded. Toole couldn't see them but he knew it.

"How did you know?" Attabury asked. "Everything was lost when you said my name."

"The law finds things out."

"Drogovich guessed," Attabury said bitterly.

"All of you men. Go to the fire." Toole watched them collect around a few orange embers that still glowed. "Put wood on," he said. One did. A flame swiftly built up.

"Miss Drogovich, please collect their weapons and bring them to me. Be careful. Don't let them grab you."

"No," she said.

"You're freed now. There's no more danger, Miss Drogovich."

"No," she said. "Have one of your posse do it."

Toole debated, and then replied. "I'm alone," he said.

He saw the men around the wavering fire exchange glances of dismay.

She turned to them. "You heard him. Or are you going to muff this one too?"

That puzzled Santiago all the more. No one moved. She waited—for what, he didn't know. Then she stooped over and picked up a rifle. Too late, he saw it swooping upward, its muzzle swinging toward him. He didn't understand. But he reacted. He kicked his stallion straight toward her. His horse bowled into her, sending her sprawling.

He couldn't believe it. He watched her roll and halt on all fours, and then stand slowly. The rifle had been knocked from her grasp.

"Miss Drogovich, you don't seem to understand. I'm Sheriff Toole. I came to free you and arrest these train robbers and abductors."

"Ow! You would, wouldn't you?"

Toole was mystified. He'd sort it out later. For now he would have to treat her as one of the gang. Perhaps she was. Perhaps she always had been; a decoy from the beginning. He'd find out soon enough. He had to find a way to collect weapons, get horses, load packs and saddles, and escort this large outfit back. All alone.

"Where's the bullion?" he asked Attabury.

The man pointed at several panniers.

"Where's the other stuff? Taken from a lot of poor miserable passengers?"

Attabury pointed at some flour sacks. "I can explain," he said. "These men are all innocent. I'm the one who's guilty. It's all my doing. I coerced them. I'll explain all that—"

"Elwood, stop being noble," Filomena snapped.

Toole noticed that she'd addressed him familiarly. So she was a part of them after all. It flabbergasted him. And yet none, save her, showed the least resistance. Amateur bandits usually didn't, he thought. His own authority as a sheriff—plus the revolver in his hand—would suffice. He hated the thought of having to fire it at sheep like these.

"They don't deserve—" Attabury began. But she shushed him.

"My father destroyed all these men," she said to Toole. "I know the whole story. If you want to arrest someone, arrest him. He stole the Fate Mine from Elwood. He bought judges and police. He hired a private army to bust heads and break arms. He employed a bunch of slimy lawyers. He bought a little land next to the Fate and had a judge rule that the veins apexed there, and everything was his. He paid the county commissioners to look the other way. He sent his thugs out. They beat up these men, broke bones, made them unfit to work anymore. My father tried to bribe Angus Dillingham there—he was the Fate's trusted accountant. But that man you're about to arrest couldn't be bought. His soul was too large. So my father destroyed him. What are victims to do when the deck is stacked? The officials are bought? The judges are corrupt? A private army roams freely, terrifying and beating whoever they choose? What are they to do after their arms are broken, their fingers smashed, their families threatened, their reputations ruined? They did what they could—and that only to start over again somewhere."

Toole sighed. "Miss Drogovich, that's a matter for a judge, not a sheriff. It may mitigate the sentencing. Our district judge—Pericles Shaw—is a man with a keen sense of justice. He'll consider the matter carefully. But that doesn't relieve me of the obligation to arrest them all for robbery, murder, abduction, property damage, and a few other things."

"It's not just," she snapped.

"Are you a part of them? Were you in on this?"

"I am now."

That wasn't an answer. "Were you in on this before-hand?"

"No. I wish I had been. And I'm in on it now. I'm going to resist arrest." She walked freely toward the horses, knowing he wouldn't shoot her, and lifted a saddle blanket and saddle to one. "I'm leaving you, Sheriff," she said.

"Stop!"

"I'm the victim, remember? You have no right to hold me. I'll do exactly as I please."

"You'll come along with me, Miss Drogovich. To answer a lot of questions if nothing else. I can legally compel that. You've made yourself a suspect. And an accessory."

Filomena Drogovich laughed and went right on saddling up.

Chapter 18

Even as Santiago stared, Filomena saddled and bridled a horse.

"Miss Drogovich," he said gently. "I'm riding a fast thoroughbred."

She turned, studied the horseflesh under Santiago with a practiced eye, and gave up. "All right. You win," she said wearily. "Sheriffs have to be sheriffs. Dogs have to be dogs."

He ignored that. "Saddle the others," he said.

"Why should I?"

A good question. "You," he said, pointing at one of them. He couldn't remember which. "Help her."

He thought it was the one called Chico. The man saddled expertly while he waited and watched in the wavering yellow glow of the fire.

"Load the bullion," Toole said. "And the rest."

The man did, wrestling the heavy panniers onto the animals.

"Load the rifles and revolvers. I'm watching you."

The man glanced at him fearfully, noting that the bore of Santiago's revolver aimed at him. Carefully, his gaze darting toward Toole, he lifted the weapons one by one from the grass and slid them into a large pannier on a packhorse. No one resisted or even looked like he might. The fight had gone out of them all: naming their names had been enough.

"All right. Mount your horses. Whoever handled the packhorses before, do it now. Head downriver." He eyed the sky uneasily, seeing no moon. If they chose to bolt and scatter in the deep dark away from the fire, he'd lose most of them. It was a risk. He thought of tying their hands and leading some of their horses on a picket line, but decided it wasn't necessary. These weren't real bad men.

They stared at him with such deep dejection and suffering engraving their faces in the firelight that he momentarily pitied them. But the memory of the dead expressman hardened him.

"All right. Stay bunched. Take your time. Anyone drifting away could get shot. I'll be behind you. Attabury, I want you with me. Miss Drogovich, you also."

And so they began, picking their way slowly eastward through a silent and solemn night. Santiago blessed his good night vision. He could see most of them ahead. On his left the inky river occasionally threw off a pinprick of starlight.

They picked their way through blackness in eerie silence. Santiago knew what they were thinking: they had each thrown away a good life and a chance to start over—for nothing. Two wrongs never made a right. Robbing their robber and tormentor might seem morally just, but it didn't satisfy the cold, hard law. And they'd gone beyond that—into the realm of robbing innocents. And murder. He wondered how it must feel to face all that. These were reputable men who'd committed a criminal act. There was a difference, and their circumstances were tragic. He'd planned to question Attabury as they rode, but found himself respecting their grief. There'd be time for questions later, and it'd help to have Manny listening and witnessing.

"There won't be a trial," Filomena said, startling him slightly. "And they won't live. You know that, but that won't stop you." A bitterness suffused her words.

"I'm afraid I don't understand, Miss Drogovich."

"You're so polite. Lace-curtain."

"That doesn't enlighten me."

"My father."

Her father. He had an inkling of her thoughts. It still surprised him to find her on the side of these men. Had she nursed some deep hatred of her father?

"What about him?"

"Do you think he'll permit a trial? Do you know how much he's got to hide? Do you know how many officials have something to hide? Do you know what his little army can do? Of course not. I wouldn't expect some dumb county sheriff to know. Well, I'll tell you. You'll put them in your little jail. There'll be a trial scheduled. And while all the lawyers are at work, an army'll come to Miles City. Not just my father's. A lot of officials have a lot to hide. In case you haven't figured it out, every one of these men is doomed. There'll be no trial."

"What do you expect them to do?"

"Try to bribe you and everyone in your county. Try to spring the prisoners with—whatever you call them—that get them out on bail. And once they're out—no one'll ever see them again. And if that fails, they'll do what they have to. You won't live; your guards won't either. My father's money talks."

"I intend to arrest him. He's abducted my wife."

She laughed harshly. "You'll die trying. And so'll your wife."

Mimi. The thought of her quieted him. Was she still in Bighorn? Would he ever see her again—alive? No doubt about it: he'd have to turn over these prisoners to Drogovich if he ever hoped to free her. And even then he wasn't certain— she'd be a witness to a lot of things he would rather keep private. A bitterness welled through him.

He found her observing him closely through the dark. "Well," she mocked, "it's finally gotten into your thick head."

He rode silently, his mind desperately chewing on a dilemma he couldn't solve, questions of justice shoved aside by the terrible realities. Mimi, Mimi. Drogovich's lever. Release the prisoners to Drogovich, he'd say, or live the rest of your life alone, Dr. Toole. The threat sickened Santiago. Mimi, Mimi, innocent, beautiful of soul and body, and doomed. He understood perfectly: no one would much care what happened to some half-breed—except Santiago. She made a perfect hostage.

"Yes," he said, "it's in my head. I suppose you have advice for me. I hear you have a large supply of it."

"Be a man! Be as much of a man as him." She pointed at Elwood Attabury III.

"That's mighty fine advice," he said.

She laughed harshly again.

He'd meant it as a joke, but the odd thing was that the advice seemed good. He accepted it fatalistically, knowing that he too was doomed; that Mimi was doomed; that these men were doomed. Maybe the two railroad detectives too. An Irish fatalism drifted through him: carry it out to the bitter end. Just as his Celtic people had carried it out to the bitter end in the face of unmovable British oppression that lay like stone over his land. Do what he had to and die.

"You've helped me more than you know," he said to her.

"Let them go now. You never captured them. You don't know their names. Let them go to Helena, gather their few things and their families and flee. You must!"

He shook his head and then realized she couldn't see that. "No," he said softly. "It's in me to play it out."

"Irish!" she exclaimed. "You want to be a ballad, that's all. You want them to sing your song in the pubs. The Ballad of Santiago Toole, and how you died. You want to be a martyr. You Irish!"

She had it right, but there was more. He had to do what he had to do, even if it was a one-man attack on an army. Even if it was irrational by all the standards of prudence. No Irishman had ever been accused of prudence, he thought. And glory to God for that.

"What do you want, Attabury?" he asked.

"To do what's right."

"And what'd that be?"

"To serve my time. Take the guilt on myself where it belongs. Return everything to the passengers. We'd decided on that anyway. We were going to sort of lose the stuff where it'd be found by officials. If I could—if I could have a miracle—I'd want these others freed and the whole guilt on me. They have wives and children waiting for them. And broken bones and crushed hands to keep them from making a living in the mines. But the West is a place for second chances. They could homestead—if they were free, without criminal records.''

Toole grieved. He couldn't do that. Neither could he answer the earnest man riding beside him. He found himself suffering as much as he ever had. These men. Victims and transgressors. The law. His oath of office to enforce it no matter what. Mimi, an innocent bystander, hostage, and half-breed. He felt himself caught in a spider's web. Things were in motion he couldn't stop or change.

"The saints preserve us," he said.

Filomena laughed.

They rode quietly into the parkland where Toole had left Manny Claghorne, or at least Toole thought it was the place. In the darkness one couldn't be sure. Manny had had a point. Toole could lose him easily in an aching void of night and wilderness. And one of these bankside flats looked much the same as another.

"We'll halt here," he said.

The caravan edged to a stop.

"Wait," he told them, wondering if they'd break. He heeled his stallion around them and edged forward, seeing nothing.

"Manny," he said softly.

"Lift them arms, I got ya covered."

"Manny! Ya idjit!"

A shot erupted.

"It's me, dammit."

"Toole? Toole? Who's them?"

"Our prisoners."

"Aw. Aw. What're you? Some kind of sheriff or something?"

"Manny. Put that piece away and get your nag."

"I gotta ride? I'll walk. If them crooks make remarks, I'll blow 'em out of the saddle."

"Manny. Get that horse and come here. We've got to make some plans."

"I don't believe it, Toole," the dick muttered. "Where's the woman?"

"I switched sides," she said.

That stopped Manny in his tracks.

The ferryman reeled them across the Yellowstone late one afternoon. The prisoners had been no problem the long way back and now stood meekly, viewing Miles City across the water. Santiago studied Miles for other reasons and was rewarded by the sight of a man in a derby hurrying away from the ferry landing. Drogovich was back, then. And the roads were being watched.

The ferry thudded to a stop against a log ramp, and Toole watched sharply as horses and people stepped gingerly to land.

"That'll be fifty cents a horse and two bits a man, Sheriff. Them's your prisoners I take it."

"Bill the county."

"Bill the county! Bill the county! A man oughter get paid within six months of when he works."

But Santiago Toole's mind was on other matters. Such as ambush. Protecting prisoners. Deciding what to do about Filomena. Getting indictments. Telling Chang Loon there'd be prisoners to feed. And above all, Mimi, Mimi. If Drogovich was back, he'd probably released her. She was of no use to him as a hostage now. . . .

But even as he thought it, he rejected it. He knew, intuitively, what Drogovich would do: try to exchange Mimi for the prisoners. And Toole knew what he wouldn't do. Drogovich would not get his hands on the prisoners, no matter—no matter. He refused to think the rest: no matter what happened to her.

"Manny—keep a sharp eye."

"I saw the bugger. Drogovich's man."

"He's back. He'll be wanting to do a deal."

"Toole—he's got an army. He don't need no deal. You oughter have a shotgun."

The prisoners looked frightened.

"Dr. Toole," Elwood Attabury said. "I'll plead guilty. I don't want a trial. I'm responsible. Tell Drogovich there'll be no trial, no publicity—"

"Hurry along," Toole snapped. He'd grown weary of gentleman bandits. He pushed them ruthlessly toward Main Street and the jail, his gaze upon every rooftop and window and door. But they reached the jail without incident.

"Manny—stand here and keep an eye peeled. The rest of you—dismount and carry everything inside. Fast."

Toole found the door locked. Pike Garrison wasn't around. He fumbled for his key, opened the door, and herded them all into the gloomy building. He unlocked the cell-room door and hustled them back, shoving them two at a time into the cells. They were as docile as sheep. It annoyed him somehow. He slammed the iron doors shut and locked them. Then he dragged the heavy packs of bullion from his front office into an empty cell, sweating as he worked. He added the sacks of valuables stolen from the passengers, and swung the cell door and locked it.

"Well?" Filomena said.

"You're free."

"I'm an accessory. You said so yourself."

He'd thought about that during the long ride home. She was simply a young woman who'd been swayed by a story of injustice. He had no intention of pressing charges for one brief episode.

"Go."

Even in the gloom, the fire of her hair made her breathtaking. He surveyed her ragged clothes and grimy flesh. "You'll want to bathe and change and find your father."

"No, not really. Is there pen and ink at your desk? I'm a witness, you know. I'll write my story."

"No," he said, remembering the shotguns and rifles on the wall racks. The hideout revolver in his desk drawer. "I want you out of here. I have things to do."

He herded her into the street and closed and locked the door. Manny had tied the horses to the hitchrail in front.

"Manny, I have to run some errands."

"Yeah. See if the little woman's okay."

"I don't think anyone'll break in here. At least not now. I'd like you to go on over to the railroad station. See what's there. Take Miss Drogovich with you. Find your other man—Biddle. Talk to Clewes—he's the night telegraph man. Grab the flimsies off his spindle. I want to read them."

"Where'll you be?"

"My house first. Then I have to find Pike Garrison—my deputy. He's city marshal too."

"Stay alive, Toole."

Filomena objected. "I don't want to be taken to my father."

"Yer comin'," Claghorne said.

"I'm of age and free."

She was right, but Toole didn't care. He'd thought at one point of using her as an ace: Filomena for Mimi. But he'd rejected it. If he wasn't going to charge her with any crime, then he wasn't going to hold her. There were right ways to enforce the law, and wrong ways.

He watched Manny clasp a meaty hand upon her arm and steer her toward the station. Then he raced toward Pleasant Street and his cottage, hoping desperately to find Mimi there. He ran, forcing his weary heart and lungs to pump blood and air to his legs. Mimi, Mimi.

He bulled through the white gate in his picket fence and bolted into his office, finding only gloom there and the dank smell of an unused building. He knew.

He tore into their private rooms looking frantically in the parlor and alcove and kitchen and bedroom and rear porch. No one. He sprang into his weedy backyard to the outhouse.

"Mimi!" he cried in silence.

He raced to his carriage barn and peered in. He spotted fresh hay in the manger of his carriage horse. Garrison had fed and watered the horse as usual. And no Mimi.

No Mimi. He'd expected that, but the actuality of it hurt.

He'd have to face Drogovich, then. He'd listen to the sinister gold baron offer to exchange her for the prisoners and more: Drogovich would want to keep the wraps on the whole business. Toole knew what his answer would be, and hated it.

He refused to think about it. Instead, he loped toward Pike's little cottage near the sporting district and found the city marshal cleaning his revolver.

"Toole. You're back."

"I've got the robbers and the girl. Need you at the jail."

Garrison absorbed that. "Trouble?"

"I'm expecting it."

"Drogovich?"

"You tell me. You're the one who'd know."

"He's here. On the siding. That boxcar, coach, and crummy are on the siding at the station along with a fancy hotel car they brought in. His men are in there."

"Where's Mimi?"

"Don't know."

"Tell me, man."

"They don't let me near them cars. They don't even let me get into the station to wire for help. They don't let Clewes or Varney wire anyone. They patrol around in pairs, keeping an eye on the jail."

"Looking for me."

"I reckon. They got men posted on the roads too."

"I saw one at the ferry."

"This town's locked up, Toole."

"Go find Chang Loon and have him feed the prisoners. Then go guard the jail. Have Blue over at the livery stable pick up the horses. They're evidence."

One-Word Garrison assembled his shooter and stood. "Where'll you be?"

"At the station."

"Don't go there alone."

"I have to."

"Your funeral. Or theirs."

"You mean my prisoners?"

Garrison nodded. "You gonna get around to telling me who they be? How you got 'em?"

"They'll tell you themselves. Go listen."

"They the ones Drogovich wants?"

"The same. I won't let it happen."

"It'll happen if you walk into the station alone."

"I'll take my chances."

Garrison nodded, looking skeptical. The man had expended more words in two minutes than he usually emitted in two days.

Toole stepped into the quiet of a late afternoon. It occurred to him that he was starved. He could scarcely remember what day it was. He cut down Sixth to Pacific Avenue and the station, intending to survey things from a distance first. He spotted Drogovich's floating lair at once. It was a luxurious hotel car of some sort, lacquered maroon, with the word SHENANDOAH gilded on its side. It had been coupled to the immigrant coach. A green-enameled, diamond-stacked engine huffed quietly, steam up, the white flags of a special in their brackets. Behind the private car stood the caboose. The shades of the private car were drawn. The immigrant coach had none, and Toole could see no one inside. Two of Drogovich's uglies lounged on the vestibule of the Palace car. The train was pointed west: Drogovich was planning to go back to Helena.

Toole wandered into the station and into the telegraph room. Varney, the day man, sat stiffly. No flimsies hung from the spindle beside the telegrapher's key. Two of Drogovich's uglies grinned at him but said nothing. Toole knew better than to wire for help.

He saw no sign of Manny or Filomena. She'd be aboard the train, probably. He didn't expect to see Mimi, but he studied the train anyway, his gaze drawn to the car with the drawn shades. An anger built in him, a regular Irish rage he couldn't choke down.

It was time to go after Drogovich. He hitched his grimy britches and hiked straight toward the vestibule at the rear of the car, where the two uglies picked their teeth.

Chapter 19

Ingmar Drogovich sat in the plush armchair surveying his daughter. She looked weary and trail-grimed. Her hair hung in greasy strings. But otherwise she looked well enough. She had a defiant glare in her eyes. He guessed what had happened at once.

"Tell me," he said.

"I wish to freshen myself."

"Your suite's back there. Along with a water closet and bath. That can wait."

"I'm dirty. You're dirty."

"Ah," he said.

She seemed reluctant to talk, so he questioned her, swiftly learning that Con Luce had died; the rest were in Toole's jail along with the bullion and valuables stolen from passengers. He learned also that Attabury had confessed and would plead guilty—along with the rest. There'd be no trial. He pondered that. No publicity, or very little.

"You're smitten by Elwood Attabury."

"No, not the way you think. He's a romantic fool."

"An honorable man."

She stared at him, faintly astonished, looking for some mockery in his face. It wasn't there. He smiled slightly.

"I feel dirty."

"You've spent my dirty money fast enough."

"I hadn't thought about it."

"And now you have. Attabury's a charming man."

"I'm going to go live with Mother."

"No more parties in Helena. No more snippy talk about all the callow swains you despise."

"I've met men. Elwood's a man—no matter what else he is. So is Toole. So is everyone who came with Elwood."

"I see. Drogovich is no longer good enough for his daughter. The humblest miner is better. He labors and toils and sweats for his pennies. But Drogovich has no soul and a heart of brass."

"You always talk like that when you don't want to own up to what you do."

He laughed softly. "Go clean up. I'll think about it."

"I'm of age and free."

"I'll think about it."

He watched her push aside the gold-tasseled red velvet drapery and head for her room. She'd find her clothing there. The black porter who came with the coach had already started drawing hot water for her. She would be clean. Cleaner than Drogovich.

He lifted the shade a little, peering up Sixth Street. Toole would be along soon enough. One could always count on Toole. Doctors and sheriffs had their ways. Unlike women. Go to her mother. Filomena reminded him not of her mother, but her grandmother—Drogovich's gaunt Danish mother. Same glowing gold hair and chiseled face. And now, the same haunting stare. He saw his mother often, her stare fixing on him from wherever she was. And now Filomena had that stare.

The palace car felt close and hot even though the ceiling vents were wide open, sucking heat out. He leaked sweat. Macqueen House might have been more comfortable. He pondered the next step. It was tempting to go. The bullion would follow him back to Helena soon enough, safer in Toole's hands than anywhere else. He'd have to weigh and inventory it first. Evidence, of course. Yes, go. Forget about Attabury. The man disappointed him. The jack of diamonds was really a five spot. Too nice. Too full of his own guilt even to demand a trial and shout to the judge and jury and press about Drogovich.

"Jason," he said. "Tell them to go."

But the porter had vanished somewhere down the long corridor. Where was Carp? He lifted the heavy shade again, looking for his gaunt lieutenant, and instead saw Toole across Pacific Avenue staring at the Palace car. Very well, then. Drogovich rose heavily and lumbered through the salon, past the rosewood bar, through a passage beside the galley, to the rear vestibule where two of his gents cleaned fingernails. That's what they did: cleaned fingernails and picked teeth, attending to exterior things because their interiors didn't belong to them.

"Let him in. Get Carp. Get them all," Drogovich said from the shadowed doorway, and lumbered back to his swiveling easy chair, swinging it rearward to receive his guest.

He heard the mutter of talk through the closed windows and then the ring of footsteps on iron stairs. The man materialized, looking as out of place in the gilded salon as a rat. A week's growth of brown beard stubbled the sheriff's face. His clothing was trail-grimed. A fever burned in his eyes. The man bulled in, surveyed Drogovich, and loomed over him.

"Where is she?"

"Filomena? Refreshing herself."

"My wife."

"You've done well, Toole. I understand you've captured them and have my bullion at the jail. Congratulations."

"My wife."

"The breed? In the caboose."

"Get her."

"No, Toole."

The man's eyes burned. That was good. Men with burning emotions were always easier to deal with than men who were quiet and rational. Sentiment was a weakness of the Irish.

"I'm taking you in. For abducting her."

"That would be difficult, don't you think?"

"No. It'll be easy. Move."

"Toole, that won't free your wife. Nothing will. She's been used and discarded."

Drogovich watched the rage build in the doctor, blind ber-serk madness. It was predictable.

"I'll get every man," he muttered.

"Ah, Toole. No one's touched her. Drogovich used her by unburdening himself to her. She holds a different kind of seed. It must be planted in the wilderness. Say good-bye to her."

It confused Toole. He looked weary. "You're not making sense, Drogovich. But I know some things. You're under arrest and coming with me. You're going to release her. Let's go."

Drogovich didn't move.

"Move, or I'll drag you back there."

Drogovich settled back in his easy chair, knowing the sheriff wouldn't shoot. He knew the sheriff perfectly, the result of much study. The man had more scruples than At-tabury. "No, Toole," he said. "You'll bring the bullion to me first."

"No."

Drogovich sighed. "The bullion is all I want. I'd thought to take Attabury back to Helena—and the rest. Keep them quiet. But there's no need. Drogovich won't be on trial. He prefers silence. Filomena tells me they'll all plead guilty. Is that so?"

"Get her."

"Never underestimate the power of conscience. It made very bad train robbers of them." He had, though. He'd sup-posed that Elwood would fight harder and be less shamed by his little escapade. He knew the feeling. The difference be-tween him and Elwood was that he did what was necessary at all times.

"Sit down, Dr. Toole. Let me find the porter."

"No."

He heard the ringing of footsteps, and moments later Ar-nold Carp entered along with four more of his men. Toole glanced at them but revealed nothing. The sheriff's face was graven granite.

"There, Toole. We'll do it Drogovich's way. In the pocket

of your trousers, somewhere, are keys to the jail. You can surrender them or you can have them wrested from you—after you're knocked senseless.''

Toole looked trapped.

''You're thinking of drawing that revolver, aren't you? It wouldn't matter—even if you shot Drogovich. My life is ashes, Toole. I can't reconcile the parts of me, and they war upon one another. I've lost my wife and now my daughter. I assure you, what happens to me doesn't matter a bit. But it matters to you. Harm Drogovich, and you'll never see your wife again.''

Toole pulled the jail keys from his pocket and tossed them onto the Brussels carpet.

''Get the gold. Leave Attabury alone. And the rest.''

Carp wasted no time. In moments several of his men were wheeling a handcart from the station up Sixth Street toward the jail. Carp remained, lounging at the bar.

''Arnold, tell them to make steam,'' Drogovich said.

Carp vanished.

''There, Toole. You can point your weapon at me now.''

Toole didn't.

''The railroad dicks are with her, you know. Nice of you to send the other one. Claphorne? Claghorne? Whatever. They're all in the caboose under guard. You're wise to sit there. You know, Toole, Drogovich has never taken a life—so far. He's a monster. He's cheated the rich and poor. He's ruined the poor. He's ruined several of Attabury's best miners. How does any mortal with a conscience live with that, eh? He doesn't. His conscience wars inside of him so much he needs confessors. He's not a religious man, so he uses secular confessors. He confesses everything that torments him—everything. And for a while the torment ceases. But then he faces the problem of keeping them silent. Ah, Toole, how does Drogovich keep your wife silent, eh?''

Toole said nothing. But Drogovich could see the man's mind concentrating—to no avail. He was trapped by his sentiment for that breed woman.

Drogovich smiled. ''There, Toole, you're a wise fellow.

How about a drink while we wait, eh? I've a bottle of good Irish whiskey there.''

Santiago didn't know he had so much sweat in him. His shirt was drenched. It oozed from his brow and rivered down his chest. It gathered in his armpits and soaked his clothing. It rose as much from the turbid heat of the private car as from the torment of his soul and mind. He listened intently to Drogovich, knowing the man wasn't lying, knowing that his own life with Mimi hinged on what happened next; on his fathoming and outwitting the gold baron, whose own penetrating gaze rarely left Toole. He saw in Drogovich exactly what Drogovich saw in himself—a man split in two, compulsively building an empire only to compromise his soul and garner the loathing of the world, and of his own family. In other circumstances he'd pity the man; but now he wanted only to rescue Mimi. He sat opposite Drogovich, knowing his revolver was as useless to him as his appendix.

"You lack love, Drogovich."

The man nodded. "Have a drink, Toole."

"Self-hatred kills. I've seen it in my practice."

"My body tells me that every minute. Look at me: I'm ten years younger than I look."

"You could change. You've a daughter and a wife to win back."

"I envy you, Toole. I can't imagine what it's like to sleep the sleep of the innocent."

"Not innocent, Drogovich. Forgiven."

"Ah, you Irish. Born guilty, but with a church to cart it all off. I lack a church."

Filomena pushed through the tasseled red curtain. She wore a fresh frock, and her brass hair hung wet. "I'm starved," she said. "Give me anything but hardtack."

Toole discerned a change in her wrought by a bath and clean clothing and comfort. The anger she'd expressed toward her father back on the trail had vanished. He eyed Drogovich, who was studying her also. She'd slide into her old ways, Toole thought. Wealth had its compensations.

Her presence effectively stopped the conversation, and
Toole settled into his swiveling chair, studying the oiled walnut, the damask drapes, the massive mirrors, the mosaics
and frescoed ceiling. He felt the train mysteriously coming
to life, and his desperation deepened. Mimi . . . He studied
the passage to the rear—past the nickel-trimmed walnut bar
and galley to the rear vestibule—and the caboose. But the
one called Carp blocked the way.

They heard clamor outside, the rumbling of iron wheels
over gravel. Drogovich pulled the shade back slightly and
peered out. Moments later the clang of shoes on the iron
steps announced the presence of others. Sweating men
dragged the heavy panniers into the Palace car. Drogovich
motioned. The men emptied the panniers on the flowery blue
Brussels carpet. Bars of gold bullion tumbled into a glowing
heap, mesmerizing Santiago. He'd never seen so much of it.

"Any trouble?"

"Naw. Joint was empty. We chased off a Chinee. Toole's
deputy wasn't around," a florid-faced one replied.

"How'd Attabury take it?"

"You ever seen a scairt man?"

They laughed.

"All right," Drogovich said. He nodded to Carp.

"This way, Toole."

"Not until you release her."

Drogovich sighed. "Forgive Drogovich, Toole."

"You made—" . . . a deal. Toole felt his body tremble
and his pulse catapult. Uglies in cheap suits grinned. Toole
closed his eyes, recovered his senses. Get off. Wire ahead.
Stop it up the line.

Drogovich chuckled. "The line's down, Toole. Both directions. We sent the wire man home. Money always talks,
eh? But you can try if you want. We'll say good-bye now.
You're a better man than Drogovich. See the company he
keeps."

Toole found himself walking rearward over lush carpet,
Carp following. He passed the bar and the galley. He opened
the oiled walnut door to the vestibule. Two of Drogovich's

men lounged there, guarding the prisoners in the caboose. Toole's heart clattered in his chest. He stepped down, his boots ringing on the patterned steel of the stairs. No foot stool stood in the cinders, and he took the long last step down to the roadbed.

The ornate Palace car loomed above him like a walled city, the ensign of wealth and power and luxury and privilege— and immunity from the laws of the land. Ahead, steam hissed from the money-green engine. Smoke belched from its diamond stack. He saw Mimi in the window of the caboose, saw her screaming at him. Holy Mary, Mimi!

The whistle shrilled. Steam belched from the pistons. The drive wheels creaked forward. The engine yanked the slack out of the first coupling.

Toole leapt between the private car and the caboose. Above him, on the vestibule, the two uglies shouted. Toole grabbed the coupling link, praying for slack. It held the two coupling loops together. Brakemen carried hickory sticks to pound it loose or pound it down. He grabbed, hearing the slam of couplings growing taut ahead. It lifted. He yanked furiously just as the hotel car moved. The jolt caught the last inch of the link and sent it sailing. The lethal missile shot past him. He tumbled backward.

The hotel car edged forward. The caboose didn't. The link clattered into gravel.

"Hey!" one of the guards yelled as the heavy car crept ahead. They stared, paralyzed. Toole staggered to his feet, whipped out his revolver and held it on them. "Don't move," he bawled. Both men froze. The distance widened. Ten feet, twenty, fifty. Silver rail blossomed between them. Ahead, the engine wailed again, spat smoke and steam. He leveled his revolver on the diminishing targets, waiting and wondering. Fifty yards. A hundred. Then one braved his fire and dashed through the vestibule door. Toole let him.

Toole leapt up the stairs to the door of the caboose and ripped it open. Mimi and Biddle huddled at the snug table beside the little galley. Claghorne lay in a bunk. They gaped at him.

"Santo!"

"Hurry!"

They had to come out the front door. A padlock sealed the rear one. "Hurry!" he cried. They were dazed. It took them a moment to grasp it. "Hurry!"

Then Biddle sprang forward, followed by Mimi, with Claghorne last. They burst onto the caboose vestibule. Far ahead he heard a faint snapping. The remaining ugly was firing—from a hopeless distance. Mimi and the N.P. dicks clattered down the stairs and leapt into the cinders, which tore at their clothing and bloodied their palms.

"Run! Go to the jail! Arm yourselves!"

If the door was still open, he thought. He no longer had keys. Garrison had a set; Chang Loon had another.

Ahead, the train screeched slowly to a halt. Toole stood, waiting, needing to know. Then, with a clank, the Johnson bar fell into reverse and the Baldwin hissed and chuffed, its bell clanging. The train backed slowly down the siding, closing the distance to the caboose. Men in derbies crowded the vestibule.

Time to go. Toole trotted past the station toward Pacific Avenue as the special wheezed backward. He heard a screech again, turned to see, and discovered that the train had stopped well shy of the caboose. Toole continued running up Sixth Street, knowing he was within rifle shot. But then the engine whistled, and slowly Drogovich's special chuffed westward again. Toole paused, scarcely believing it. Faster and faster it went, steam shrilling from the pistons, ever westward, the engine, the boxcar, the immigrant coach—and Drogovich's private car. It swung onto the mainline and didn't pause to reset the switch. It thundered onto the trestle over the Tongue River and then vanished behind cottonwoods, its rumble still reverberating through town.

He sighed, felt his pulse slow, and shoved his sweaty revolver into its holster. He no longer saw Mimi and the two dicks: they'd reached Main and swung out of sight. A wave of weariness hit him. He couldn't run. His legs wouldn't work. But they propelled him toward the jail anyway. His soaked shirt clung like snakeskin. He reached Main and headed east toward his sheriff office and jail. Ahead, Garrison hove into view. And Chang Loon—each armed.

He raced past them, leapt up the steps and into his office. She was there, her face broken into anguish and yearning. He swept her to him.

"Santo, Santo!" she cried, meeting his lean body with hers. She snuggled into him, sobbing, clinging.

"Toole, ya done it," Manny Claghorne said joyously.

Around him the railroad detectives grabbed shotguns and shells; Garrison barricaded the jail. Chang Loon raced off to get help from merchants. Good men all. Toole scarcely noticed. The miracle of Mimi engulfed him. Her tears soaked into his shirt, and her sobs wrenched him. He caressed her hair and pulled her tighter to him. It wasn't really a time for tears.

Chapter 20

Pericles Shaw looked unusually solemn, Santiago thought. The judge had even scraped his whiskers and put on his good suit. He settled himself in his squeaking chair and peered over the assemblage like a bullfrog, which he distinctly resembled. A scholarly bullfrog wearing gold-rimmed half glasses.

The spectators sat down again.

"This court is now in session," he said, glancing at the clerk and at Pike Garrison, who was acting as bailiff. The windows were open, admitting a breeze and flies as usual. The carcasses of innumerable flies lay on the gritty floor of the chamber. Toole slid his hand into Mimi's and waited.

"Defendants will rise for sentencing," Pericles said with that gravelly voice Toole had heard for so many years.

Elwood rose, followed by the others. They looked pale, as much from not seeing the sun as from the dread that weighed on them. Elwood looked dapper in suit and cravat, his hair slicked down, his patrician face grave and dignified. The rest, less well shaven and shorn, their hands hard and brown and battered from life's toil, their clothing rough, seemed less confident and far more frightened.

Shaw shuffled some papers, and then peered up at them over his half spectacles. "The bills of indictment vary somewhat from man to man. Collectively, there were thirty-nine charges of armed robbery involving railroad passengers and the conductor. One charge of assault with a deadly weapon involving a passenger. One charge of murder in the first degree—all murders done in the commission of a crime are murders in the first degree. In addition, there are charges against the destruction of property; wrecking the express car; destroying the strongboxes. In addition there is the charge of abduction involving a victim's daughter. There are some lesser charges as well that I won't go into here; they're public record.''

All in all, Toole thought, a formidable battery of indictments facing some gentlemanly bandits.

"At the preliminary hearing," Pericles Shaw continued, "you all pleaded guilty and acknowledged the confessions you each drafted and signed. Now, ah, for the record, do any of you wish to change those confessions, add or subtract, recant? Do any of you believe they were supplied under duress?"

He waited. The prisoners stood silently, saying nothing.

"Very well, then. This court takes your silence as an affirmation that your signed confessions were voluntarily submitted and are accurate in every detail."

Toole peered around. Few spectators had come. But the wives of the accused sat behind him, red-eyed and miserable. The public had long since lost interest in the robbery. Some reporters were on hand, though, scribbling in their notebooks.

"This court urged upon you to obtain lawyers, individually or severally, and informed you that upon signing an affidavit of poverty, the court would engage an attorney for anyone who so desired. I regret that you didn't. You jointly chose to throw yourselves upon the mercy of this court. Attorneys might have illuminated things I have not seen or understood. I've weighed matters according to my concepts of justice, and if you are so inclined, it is not too late to hire an attorney and appeal."

Again, silence. Toole picked up a harshness in Pericles's tone and wondered about it.

"Very well, then; we'll proceed. There are matters to discuss here; matters that bear upon my sentencing. Your various confessions alluded to the armed robbery of passengers

as camouflage, something to conceal the true purpose of this
affair. Your confessions emphasized that you'd decided to
return this booty, making it appear to have been lost in flight,
and therefore this robbery of thirty-nine passengers and Conductor Graves ought not to be taken seriously by the court.
Well, this court takes it seriously indeed. Quite apart from
the stupidity of trying to camouflage one crime with thirty-
nine others, I find no reason for lenience in the notion that
you intended to return the stolen goods. That does not make
these thirty-nine acts of banditry any less an offense against
humanity.''

Toole knew it'd go hard on them. Pericles was baring fangs,
and perhaps rightly so.

''I've examined the roster of stolen goods. Cash, wedding
rings, heirloom pocket watches engraved on their backs, jew-
els. Even a sheaf of shares in various corporations. But most
of all, cash, even pennies. You left those passengers bereft,
helpless, far from home. Were it not for the generosity of the
Northern Pacific Railroad and the Western Union Telegraph
Company, these victimized mortals would have been without
food and shelter and the means to get help. As it was, the
N.P. footed the bill for meals and hotel rooms. Some camouflage.''

All of them looked crestfallen, Dillingham more so than
the others. Astleheim peered into space. Enrico Ferrero
stared at the floor.

''The law finds no merit in this alleged plan to return the
wealth, and neither does this court. That it was done for the
alleged purpose of camouflaging a crime only makes matters
worse.''

The judge sipped from a tumbler of water and plowed on
relentlessly. ''Each of you alleges that you were driven to
these desperate acts by the suffering and injustice you re-
ceived at the hand of Ingmar Drogovich. I don't know the
truth of these allegations. Mr. Drogovich is not on trial here.
If all this is true, you have my sympathies—to some extent.
You suffered at the hands of this man. But your plea for
mercy on that account does not have merit in this court, and

neither does your plea for mercy grounded on the undeniable truth that you've lived upright lives prior to this business. If you've lived exemplary lives, it is a clear sign that you've always known right from wrong, good from evil. You are adult men, all of sound mind. You each made a conscious and informed choice. I will do you the honor of supposing you understood the nature of your deeds even before you did them. Indeed, your confessions describe at length the planning you engaged in, and the sense that robbing the robber would at least partly even the scales. This court—and the law—disagree."

Throwing the book at them, Santiago thought. That was like Pericles. He could go either way. Give him a genuinely mitigating circumstance and he'd be the soul of kindness.

"Let's proceed now to a few words about the victims. I've been in touch with the passenger who suffered the concussion as a result of a pistol-whipping. He is not yet healed; suffers acute headaches, depression, and deteriorated vision which his physician believes may be permanent. A life has been gravely damaged, all for the frivolous and criminal purpose of camouflaging another crime."

Ferrero swallowed and stared at the floor.

"Now a word about the other victim—the one from whom life has fled. His name was Clinton Hodgpeth; age at death, thirty-three."

Pericles paused.

"He'd been with the express company since the age of sixteen, advancing steadily, promoted because of his graciousness with customers, flawless recordkeeping and delivery of parcels, and overall excellence. The company advanced his salary seven times and had singled him out for future managerial tasks. Clinton had a bright future."

The judge paused again.

"His widow, they tell me, is inconsolable there in Bismarck. She has three children to care for. The railroad told me something of great interest. Mrs. Hodgpeth is totally blind in one eye, almost blind in the other. She sees light and darkness and a few blurred forms. Until Clinton came along, she despaired of her life. But he did come along, told her she was beautiful of form and spirit. He told her he loved her for herself; but she protested that he was proposing because of pity; he assured her he wasn't—he'd never met a woman so lovely and courageous. Well, I needn't elaborate. He brought light and love to Clara Hodgpeth. His killers plunged her into eternal night. The express company has arranged a small pension—but that's all in the world she possesses, save for the love of her children."

"Oh, Santo, Santo," Mimi whispered.

The judge glared at her, wanting silence.

Elwood Attabury swallowed hard and stared ahead. He looked a lot less assured than when he'd been marched in by the bailiff.

"Mr. Attabury, step forward, please."

Attabury did, slowly.

"Apparently you didn't pull the trigger. But by your own admission you planned all this, recruited everyone, acquired horses and weapons. The law holds that you are exactly as guilty as the the one who pulled the trigger. You were present: you and Constantine Luce and Karl Astleheim. You three formed the bullion squad. You blew the door, killed Hodgpeth, and blew the strongboxes. You three committed first-degree murder."

Elwood Attabury sagged.

"My presentencing inquiries led me to the discovery that you come from what is known as a nice family in Boston. You were the child of privilege, schooled and trained and civilized; taught moral and ethical matters by doting parents. You, above all, knew precisely the nature of your acts—but you made the conscious choice to do them; to throw aside the whole weight of your upbringing. It makes it all the harder for me to sympathize with you. You've pleaded for clemency on that very ground—good family, upright conduct heretofore. But it's a poor ground, I'd say. It damns you the more."

Attabury began to step back into the line but the judge stayed him. "Mr. Attabury, you made much in your confession of the idea that you'd exhausted all remedies; that you could find no justice from a corrupt court in Lewis and Clark County, corrupted police, corrupted officials, and a mendacious press, and that's why you resorted to—crime as a form of restitution. Well, sir, I beg to differ. By your own admission, these were all the avenues you tried. Helena is the capital of the territory; in it resides a territorial governor you didn't go to see; an attorney general you didn't visit. Politicians and officials you never talked to. There were, and are, a dozen other influential papers in the territory entirely uninfluenced by Mr. Drogovich. You contacted none of them. You failed to bring suit in a different venue. Isn't that so?" Attabury nodded; the judge plunged into his discourse again. "It's so. The truth is—you took a fancy to the robbery idea, and delighted in it."

That observation struck the bone of it, Toole thought. Pericles Shaw had penetrated to the bottom of it, to the soul of Elwood Attabury III. Around him, the reporters scribbled furiously, catching the importance of all that.

"I'm done with my remarks. Enrico Ferrero, step forward and receive your sentence. You are hereby sentenced to six months apiece for thirty-nine counts of armed robbery, to be served consecutively at the territorial penitentiary in Deer Lodge. Plus two additional years for assault with a deadly weapon."

One by one Pericles sentenced them all. Chico, the horse handler, got the least—twelve years. Ferrero and Dillingham twenty and eighteen. Astleheim life imprisonment for firstdegree murder and the rest.

That left Elwood Attabury III twitching before the judge.

Pericles sighed unhappily. "I've agonized about your case the most of all. I've weighed your arguments and pleas and find they actually go against you. You're the mastermind of a robbery and murder; a source of deep suffering. You've betrayed your upbringing. Your defenses fall to pieces.

"Elwood Attabury the Third, I herewith sentence you to hang by the neck until dead, at sunrise, September the eighth, eighteen and eighty-four."

People gasped.

Elwood Attabury III seemed to fold into himself like a withering orchid.

Holy Mary, Santiago thought, pitying the man. He grieved. Was this justice? He wondered how he'd ever spring the gallows trap on a lad he still admired. He knew he couldn't.

"It's the wrong man," Mimi hissed.

Women wept. Reporters clambered to their feet, wanting to interview the defendants. The bailiff shouted. Slowly Santiago stood, shaken to his marrow, a dread building in him about the duties he couldn't perform. He would have to resign.

"Order!" Pericles cried. "Order!" He hammered the scarred desk with the butt of his revolver. "This court is in session. Bailiff, seat them all!"

Santiago sank into his seat, and the others slowly settled into theirs. Beside him Mimi shed tears.

"Now then. Sentences suspended pending good behavior."

Time froze. Breath stopped. The drone of a bee in the room seemed loud.

"I will define good behavior. As long as you behave in the manner I shall define, your sentences will remain suspended. If you falter, your sentences will be carried out at once."

Attabury looked so dazed that Santiago wondered whether he even grasped this turn of events. The rest looked numb and uncertain.

"I am interested in retribution. Repayment is the proper punishment for amateur bandits. Mr. Attabury, step forward again."

Elwood Attabury had to be lifted from his bench and steered forward by his fellow defendants, but at last he stood alone.

"Good behavior shall be the unstinting support of Mrs. Hodgpeth and her children for twenty years, even if she should remarry. You will find the means to pay her a sum of one hundred fifty dollars a month and will do so promptly on the first of each month. That is more than he earned, but

I wish to take into account his promising future. It is a miserable compensation for murder, but it means a secure life for a blind woman and her children. If you fail, your life will be required of you. Do you understand?''

Attabury nodded.

"Tell me you do, for the record."

"I do," Attabury mumbled, and wobbled back to his bench like a drunk.

One by one, old Pericles Shaw imposed his version of good behavior on the rest. In each case it would be compensation of the victims: the passengers, the railroad, the express company, the pistol-whipped man, all of the requirements carefully tailored by the thoughtful justice to fit the incomes of working men. If they failed, the judge reminded them, they'd serve their full sentences.

Santiago felt tears welling, and old Pericles seemed blurred and beautiful up there in his creaky chair. The man had fashioned his own special justice for amateur bandits, even while applying the law of the land. When at last Pericles dismissed the court, Santiago found Mimi's hand in his and walked home, drained but not saddened.

"The real criminal escaped," Mimi said, and Santiago agreed.

About the Author

Richard S. Wheeler is the Spur Award–winning author of many Westerns. *The Fate* is the fourth in his Santiago Toole series, which includes *Incident at Fort Keogh*, *The Final Tally*, and *Deuces and Ladies Wild*. Mr. Wheeler makes his home in Big Timber, Montana.